# THE
# BOARDING HOUSE
*Stories from an Irish Lodging House*

First published in 2008 by
Appletree Press Ltd
The Old Potato Station
14 Howard Street South
Belfast BT7 1AP

Tel: +44 (028) 90 24 30 74
Fax: +44 (028) 90 24 67 56
Email: reception@appletree.ie
Web: www.appletree.ie

**The Boarding House – Stories From an Irish Lodging House**

A catalogue record for this book is available from the British Library.

ISBN-13: 978 1 84758 086 3

Desk & Marketing Editor: Jean Brown
Copy-editing: Jim Black
Cover Design: Stuart Wilkinson
Production Manager: Paul McAvoy

9 8 7 6 5 4 3 2 1

AP3534

# THE
# BOARDING HOUSE

*Stories from an Irish Lodging House*

Peggy McFeely

Appletree Press

To all the people who touched my life – making it a splendid one

# Contents

# CHAPTER ONE

## Sunday Worship

Miss Evelyn Tracey nodded to the other parishioners as she made her way to her pew in the old country church. Her head, with its iron grey hair neatly plaited into a magnificent 'bun', carried a hat that was fashionable yet sedate.

She dabbed at the tiny beads of perspiration on her brow and upper lip with a lace edged handkerchief, her cheeks pink from the walk to her place of worship. She savoured the familiar smells that are peculiar to Presbyterian churches. The wooden pews had their own perfume. There were polish and soap smells and the citrus bouquet from the orange blossom arrangements at the pulpit wafted over the congregation. Sunlight streamed across the communion table, lighting the flowers there like a heavenly spotlight.

Miss Tracey noted each member of the congregation as they walked quietly to their family pews. She always arrived early to observe her fellow worshippers. She had a withdrawn, reserved personality and an accompanying avid curiosity about her fellow creatures. During the rather uncomfortable period before the service when only three or four sat in each pew, any noise at all was clearly noted. She could hear who had a troublesome cough, who ate sweets. She strained to listen to loud whispers between family members, to catch a bit of gossip.

She watched the 'style' as she called it, as the ladies moved up the aisle, and she talked to herself, keeping up a running commentary regarding the efforts of these matrons to be fashionable.

'Mary Crampsie out again in a dress too tight for her sonsy figure – just fair sweeled up in it,' she thought as she watched her progress up the aisle. 'After six weans what could you expect?' As she noted her crab-like gait, she thought 'Isn't she badly travelled?"

Miss Tracey observed her own trim ankles and placed her polished shoes on the tapestry footstool. There was an aura of maidenly innocence about her. Her blouses were always snowy white, with perfectly ironed reveres. Her nails were buffed to a high polish and her few pieces of jewellery discreet.

She sat alone, the rest of the pew empty. She allowed the sound of gentle stillness, before the minister would rise to open the service, to envelop her. She thought of the cake she had left to cool in the pantry, the strawberries waiting with cream to decorate it. Her thoughts were interrupted by Mrs Crawford turning around to whisper to her that she would be needed to help at the 'social' in the coming week. Mrs Crawford had facial hair, and had done nothing about it. Miss Tracey tried not to notice, but the tufted upper lip fascinated her. Mrs Crawford had concentrated on her greying hair, dyeing it a matt black which clashed with her white wrinkled face. Miss Tracey had weighed up the 'pros' and 'cons' when her own hair had started to go grey. Having viewed Mrs Crawford's white crown with gingery white showing among the black, she just thankfully allowed the grey to continue.

Her gaze went to the bulging figure of Mr Crawford. He had hair tufts in both nostrils and ears and everything about him bulged. His protruding eyes were always swivelling after the figure of the female worshippers. Miss Tracey often gazed at the pair of them, and tried to imagine them in the sexual act when they begot their four children. Thinking about this, she allowed herself to look at Mr Brown, the plumber, for just a short time. He always aroused strange feelings in her. When he came to 'plumb' for her, she couldn't stop looking at his brown forearms. She liked the way the hair grew on the backs of his hands and arms. She wanted to stroke them with her fingers. His eyes fascinated her – dark brown eyes with strange flecks – and she always found his gaze so intense that she had to look away. Oddly enough, she seemed to need the plumber quite often. She would send for him tomorrow: she had that cream cake and strawberries.

The sermon commenced and Miss Tracey turned her attention to the minister. She thought he was full of affectation, and his contrived accent irritated her. He was of the brigade that swiped a long portion of hair from the back of the head, across the bald spot in the front, and then fixed it with a shiny sticky 'glar'. She looked at the flowers to refresh her eyes and then viewed the choir. They sat with serious faces and fixed expressions, gazing over the heads of the congregation as the thundering voice of the minister broke over them.

The minister's wife sat by herself and faced them all. Miss Tracey wondered if she had to live up to the husband's sermons. 'Why did women marry ministers?' she mused. How could they bear a man around the house all day? She thought of the manse with its big rooms, big inherited furniture and the faint musky lavender-like smell that greeted the nostrils in the hallway. The wife wasn't a great baker either, and she didn't leave any impression on a person at all. She had been in tears one day when a parishioner called. It had created a great topic among the women as to why she had been crying. Ministers' wives never cried. Miss Tracey thought of the way his hair must look without the 'glar', on his pillow in the morning, and decided, as she sucked a cinnamon sweet, that the wife had plenty to cry about.

The children in the pew behind fistled with sweetie papers and began to whisper. Miss Tracey just inclined her head sideways and the fistling stopped. She was of the old breed, and they obeyed her kind of authority. She was glad she had no children. They messed up your life.

She looked out of the window and gazed at the sky and the clouds floating past. She watched an aeroplane and remembered her only love affair. It had been during the war and he had been a pilot. Her one sexual encounter had not been earthmoving. She remembered her head banging against the top of the bed, and wondered why there was so much emphasis on sex these days. She glanced at the plumber again; he was singing with the rest of the congregation. His hair curled enticingly at the nape of his neck and she enjoyed the shape of his broad back in the grey suit.

Once the service was over, Miss Tracey moved sedately to the door. She waited to shake the minister's hand, and smiled charmingly.

"I enjoyed the sermon today," she murmured. "I get so much from weekly worship."

She nodded to right and left and moved out into the warm sunshine.

The minister glanced after her. 'Such a charming lady,' he thought as she smiled back at him. He always tried to include something that would interest her in his sermons, and he felt rewarded with her sincere words and warm smile.

It was people like her who made it all worthwhile.

# CHAPTER TWO

## Miss Evelyn comes from church

Miss Evelyn smoothed the kid gloves over her fingers and moved quickly through the crowd that stood around the church door.

'What do they find to talk about?' she wondered, as she nodded to a few who turned towards her.

"How are you Miss Tracey?"

"Fine, fine," she replied smiling, but not making eye contact.

She didn't want to be drawn into conversation with these people. It could involve being asked to help at women's meetings. Watching them at church was one thing, but joining with them to actually talk to them was not to be considered.

It was a fine day and Evelyn enjoyed feeling the slight breeze and the sunshine that lit up the flowers in the gardens she passed. Her front door pleased her. The brass knocker and letterbox glittered against the red paint. She smoothed them with her gloves and frowned at the scratch marks around the keyhole. That would be the work of young Angus, a boarder who always jabbed his key around, searching for the opening. He said he wasn't drunk –he just couldn't find it.

He was one of sixteen boarders who lived with Evelyn, her sister Chrissie and their mother Annie. The hall smelled like a church. The smell of polish on the old furniture greeted her as she unpinned her hat and glanced around. Were there any more scratch marks on the hall chair? She shuddered to think of the day when she arrived home to find John Parker standing on it, facing the wall, with the phone to his ear. Her umbrella had caught him at the back of his knees and he had doubled over in pain, muttering a quick 'goodbye' to the caller.

"I can't talk on the phone unless I get up and face the wall," he told her as he sat on the chair, rubbing the calves of his legs.

"If I catch you on that chair again you won't feel like talking much anyway!" said Evelyn.

'Eejit,' she thought, 'an' him a teacher too!'

As she waded in among the boarders in the dining room her gloomy mood deepened. They were sprawled about covered with swathes of newspapers, and the fire she noted was well down.

'Too lazy to move to the peat bucket,' she thought, as she clodded on the two remaining peats. The sparks flew out, and it pleased her to see the trouser covered legs draw up sharply to avoid burning. Carrying the empty basket, Evelyn landed in the kitchen.

"Those are the laziest lot of louts lying in there. Chrissie, would you go down to the cellar for more peats? I have still got my good clothes on."

Chrissie wiped her hot face and clambered slowly down the cellar steps to the peats piled in a corner. She rapped with a stick on the ground to scatter any rat or mouse in the pile and began to fill the basket. She talked to herself about the men. They wouldn't say "Chrissie would ye need a han' with the peats?" Not them. Her legs encased in lisle stockings were sore with veins. She had to clasp the old banister as she hauled up the heavy weight.

Chrissie was heavily built. As Evelyn described her, 'she was all of a piece', square set with broad shoulders. She was a good cook and a great baker. Their mother Annie was slim and wiry, always neat. They worked well as a team. They all despised their charges, the boarders.

There was a loud yell from the dining room.

"Miss Evelyn – the room's on fire!"

The men were up flailing about with newspapers at Bob's trousers. He was dancing about, shaking his short legs and trying to quench the burning fabric.

"I'm burning alive! I'm on fire!" The paper in his hand was in flames as well.

"Keep calm!" Evelyn shouted. "Roll him on the floor out here in the hall – not on my good carpet."

Bob was rolled over and over, with hands beating away at his trouser legs.

"I'm singed! I'm singed!" he yelled.

"Calm yourself man, it's only cloth," said Evelyn.

Dickie the young boarder had reached for the big fire extinguisher and banged it on the floor. The instrument went off, doing its job, filling the air with a white thick froth which rose and rose up the staircase. Now they couldn't see. Bob was somewhere on the floor, crawling about in search of his glasses. He still had them on, but didn't realise this.

"I can't see. I can't see."

To the women this was like the end of the world. Somebody opened the front door and the white clouds wafted out. A stranger came in.

"Where's the fire? Where's the old lady? Is she safe?"

The old lady in question – Annie – was hauling the roast out of the oven. She had felt her way around the kitchen.

"It's ruined, the dinner's ruined."

The Fire Brigade arrived, and an ambulance. Bob kept protesting that he was going to die, but an examination proved that only his trousers had suffered. The fire (which had been mainly Bob) was out, so the Fire Brigade left.

"What happened?" Evelyn kept asking the rest of the men.

"Well, you know how you don't allow smoking? Well, Bob had a cigarette in his hand when you came in. He put it down by his side to hide it. The papers on his legs caught fire, and his trousers underneath. He made it worse by wafting the papers about."

Evelyn was relieved. She thought it had been a spark from the peats.

"Then who was the idiot who set off that fire extinguisher?"

Dickie admitted he knew nothing about the procedure and couldn't control the thing. As the white mist was clearing the extent of the damage could be seen. This innocent looking white stuff became black as it came in contact with anything. Even the bedrooms were full of it. The rooms and contents were covered with a greasy black gunge.

The women sat down in the kitchen.

"What'll we do?"

Their faces and hands were covered with the stuff.

"Send out for chips," Annie answered. "They can eat them out of bags. The saucepans on the cooker are full of the black stuff too. Send the Dickie one and let him pay: he caused it."

# CHAPTER THREE

## The Kitchen

The women always made for the kitchen. It was their oasis, the place where they could be together, and had grown with pieces of furniture bought from a second hand shop. Evelyn was always on the lookout for cupboards and chests of drawers to fit around the room. These were crammed with tins of food and cooking ingredients. The latest piece had a concealed ironing board, drawers lined with zinc and a top cupboard to hold all the medicines they needed. Jim the second hand man had hauled it into place, opening the ironing board part with a flourish. The big table in the centre was where they sat to talk over their problems, and also to have their endless cups of tea. Annie had a habit of swilling the last dregs of hers around and around, to the irritation of the others. Their eyes would watch the contents swirling, waiting for the liquid to spill over, but she always had control. She sucked lozenges called Chlorodynes and her breath always smelled of ether.

The boarders were not encouraged to come into the kitchen; they occupied the rest of the house and the women kept them at the kitchen door when they came to pay their weekly rent. This money was due on Fridays and Evelyn kept a book, which held their names and dates of boarding. As she passed the boarder a plate of dinner he would hand over the weekly payment, or mutter that he hadn't got the money. Her eyes would narrow and the other two would stop dishing out the food at the cooker. Evelyn would hold the plate back for a second, close to her chest as if to signify that 'no money: no food'. The plate would then be passed over with a severe look from Evelyn, and a warning that the money would need to be paid the following week. The women agreed the boarder would have to be watched. Another older man couldn't attempt to eat his dinner without a glass of buttermilk from a big jug kept in the fridge. Evelyn would forget and walk over to get the drink with slow deliberate steps. The buttermilk was handed over with a look of disdain.

"It's my old stomach, you know," he'd quaver.

"A stomach like a horse," she would inform the others when he'd closed the door.

The food was plain but well cooked. Mashed potatoes were like dollops of cream and the meat was cooked to perfection. The desserts were the old favourites, bread and butter pudding with meringue topping, gooseberry and rhubarb fools, velvety custards and shivering jellies. These were all lovingly made and well presented. Dinners were piping hot never 'caul as clash', Annie's favourite description. The women only picked at their own dinners – small plates of bits and pieces. Having worked so long with food, they weren't interested in eating hearty meals. Evelyn kept bottles of Lucozade in the fridge and drank it all day. "That'll rot yer insides," Annie would say, as Evelyn poured the orange fizzy liquid into a glass. "You sound like a sheugh gulping that stuff down." Annie had in her later years developed a fad for fish and chips, and Evelyn had to hurry to a local shop to satisfy this new hunger. She needed them 'to taste her mouth'. Chrissie was fond of bananas.

Chrissie's baking was excellent – all kinds of scones emerged from flour and buttermilk. They each took turns at their culinary tasks on the scrubbed wooden table, making the legs groan with their efforts. Annie baked the 'fadge' or potato bread and apple cakes. She also made a concoction called 'pertie pudding'. She never weighed any ingredients. She put in a 'gropin' of this or that, and she was a dab hand at sweet milk scones that she baked on the griddle. She would stop now and again to sit down and wipe the steam off her glasses, squinting as she held them up to the bright kitchen light to inspect for smears.

"It's wild warm in here – open that back door!" one would shout to the other.

Chrissie used to wonder why Evelyn never had flour flying about and over herself when she baked. They liked to watch her work at the table. The pastries and cakes she produced were works of art.

If there was a fall out between them they all had ways of showing their feelings. Whoever was baking could be hampered by the others blocking the doors to the cupboards and fridge. The kitchen was small, and elbows jutting out were sharp weapons. Feet stuck in an awkward place could trip, and essential items could disappear.

"Where is that baking soda?"

"Did anybody see the sultanas?"

The others would hurry about their business and hardly answer.

They watched with wonder as the empty plates came back from the dining room. Where do they put it all? If any of the plates had bits left on it they said that the boarder had made 'hawk's meat' of the meal.

The Aga cooker was foddered with anthracite seven times a day, and was the workhorse in charge of all cooking. Annie watched over it, 'cootering' to its every need. Lids were left down gently and only the softest cloths washed the cream body. If she could smell even a whiff of gas coming from the pipe at the wall she kept up a lament:

"What'll we do Evelyn, if the cooker goes off? Do ye now smell something?"

When a liquid substance began to foam at the opening of the pipe, the wailing would start.

"Get the man to come, we've waited too long!"

Turning the cooker off was a big event, and Annie sat in the front room whingeing and moaning as she rocked backwards and forwards, listening to the sounds from the kitchen. Willy the cooker man was sent for, and he worked with some kind of rods and brushes, clearing out liquid muck from the pipe. When it was over Annie could come back into the kitchen, smiling as she put her hand on the cooker's body to feel it heating up again. She would have paid any money to get it back to life, and was content until the next time.

The kitchen became quiet in the evenings. The kettles were boiled to fill the hot water bottles to be taken up to the boarders' beds. Chrissie always tried to hold them away from her as she trudged up the steep stairs. She could only carry three at a time on account of the heat.

"And the sods wouldn't even bring them down in the morning," she would tell the others as her nightly mission began.

The last cup of tea was drunk and pills and medicine taken. Annie and Evelyn let their hair down from their buns and slowly mounted the stairs.

# CHAPTER FOUR

## Breakfast

The next morning the women trooped into the kitchen, Evelyn in her white blouse, immaculate skirt, neat shoes and stockings. Chrissie always yawned and stumbled along. Annie wiped the table and then her chair, before sitting down to wind her hair up into a bun. She rested her arms several times before finally securing it with a big hairpin. The work of the day would begin with the rattle on the stairs of the first boarder's feet – bounding down to claim the bathroom.

"That'll be the bagpipe player. Chrissie, shout to him to go easy on the hot water. He shakes it round him like a hairy dog. Is that kettle on the boil? Is the milk at the door?"

Annie kept up the usual questions as she smoothed her apron over her dress. She yawned and yawned as she gnashed the words out

"Ye'll lose yer teeth, Mother," Chrissie told her, "if ye go on like that."

Annie never listened to her but would gaze at the cooker and watch the kettle.

"Is that cooker on? It hasn't gone out?" She'd jump up and stagger over to feel it, like a nurse testing for temperature. "Is it stoked?"

The kettle would be shifted a bit and the spout examined for steam.

"You'll fall. Catch yourself on. Sit down."

Chrissie would disappear down the cellar steps with the hod for more anthracite, her legs bending awkwardly because of their shape.

"Close that cellar door. You're letting the heat out next."

"Mother sit there and don't fash yourself at this time in the morning," said Chrissie.

By now Annie was turning around to fistle in the dresser drawer.

"Don't dare take those Regulettes on an empty stomach. You'll run your bowels out of yourself."

Evelyn took the tin containing the wee brown pills from Annie, who began to cry, screwing her face up, her small nose getting red. Evelyn slapped the pan on to heat and poured out tea for her Mother.

"Get that in you, and go easy on the sugar."

"I'd be better-off in a home," said Annie, as she spooned in sugar and wiped her eyes.

"Do you think so?"

Chrissie slammed down the hod on the top step and dragged it across the floor. She opened the flap on the cooker and lifted up the hod to begin to let the anthracite trickle in.

"This lifting will dislodge my womb," Annie announced to the other two. "Why do you never have to haul it up?" This was directed at Evelyn, standing immaculate in her white blouse and black skirt. "You are stronger than me."

Evelyn christened the pan with the first egg of the day.

"The Buttermilk Man says he wants sunny side up."

"I'll 'sunny side' him!" Evelyn slapped the turner against the side of the pan. " Put the plates into the oven to heat and make toast, mother. The bread's beside you. That teacher one wants his dry and crisp not buttered when it's hot."

"You're jokin'!"

"No. He mentioned it last night when I gave him his hot water bottle."

"What did you say?"

"I said 'I'll tell her'."

"So you have."

"Make it as usual, and the butter is beside you."

The kitchen now was alive, plates rattling, bacon sizzling – the smell of tea and coffee adding to the atmosphere in the kitchen.

Annie began to perk up.

"Can I get my Regulettes now?"

"No not yet, because the hot tea will activate them, and you'll have to be helped upstairs, and I haven't got time now."

Annie's face crumpled again.

"Quit that. There's that teacher one coming down stairs. Butter the toast."

Chrissie stood ready with a tray already holding the tea pot and toast rack, while Evelyn slid the perfectly fried egg onto a warm plate – placing rashers of bacon around it. She piled mushrooms at its side and placed scarlet tomato rings around the plate.

"That's a work of art Evelyn, far too good for that boy. He'll have half of it over the table, for he reads a book propped up on the milk jug. Such a handlin' I had yesterday when the jug toppled over – and he's a teacher too. They weren't reared – they were dragged up."

"They have no bother with their bowels anyway," Annie piped up.

"Is she getting worse?" Evelyn asked Chrissie.

Evelyn was beginning to worry about the bowel business.

"What would I do if they stopped?" whinged Annie, as she viewed the pile of toast.

# CHAPTER FIVE

## The Fridge Man

The doorbell rang and they stared at one another. The *ring* never failed to annoy them. Friends and boarders walked in – strangers used the bell. Evelyn moved slowly up the hall, the other two watching anxiously at the dark shadow etched against the glass. The figure on the doorstep, poised on tiptoes, rocked backwards and forwards. The small squat man was well enough dressed, she thought. The grey hair was raked back from a square jawed, bright red face.

"I'm looking for lodgings," he announced, rocking away on small feet.

Evelyn had drawn herself up, arms crossed, head held high so that she could look closely at this person. They had a vacancy, but had to be so particular about the kind of person allowed into the house. All depended on this interview.

"For how long?" she asked, hardly moving her lips.

"As long as I need to stay."

"What do you work at?"

"I repair fridges," replied the prospective boarder.

"Do you leave at weekends?" asked Evelyn.

"No, I need full board."

"Wait here."

Evelyn headed back to the kitchen to the other two women who waited, eyes alert, eager to hear about this stranger, this unknown person who stood at the door.

"What'll we do?" Evelyn pursed her lips. "I've a feeling he's a drinker. His skin has that fresh pinkish colour, and his nose is red. I noticed the whites of his eyes are a bit pinkish too. He's well enough dressed, but his hands and nails are rough."

"The extra money *would* be useful," they kept muttering. "What'll we do? Would he be fond of the bottle?"

"Well I couldn't ask him outright," said Evelyn.

"We have enough bother here."

The women gazed anxiously at one another.

"Do you think we're wise? Should we try him?"

Evelyn walked up the hall. She hated to take in another boarder, an unknown stranger into their lives. The kitchen door was kept open so that the other two could watch the new boarder hauling his possessions into the house and up the stairs. This was when the dislike could become a kind of hatred. The women had to hold themselves back from rushing out to shout 'No you can't take that up our stairs!'

The fishing rods and nets that he held carefully in front of him were lethal fishing tackle objects. One boarder before had kept his under the bed, and the amount of fluff gathered around the bits and pieces had caused the women to have the lot out every day to dust and brush. Then the sharp spikes of the flies left carelessly on the mantle were another hazard.

"He's a fisherman," Evelyn mouthed to the others.

They watched piles of books disappear up the stairs.

"He says he's a singer, going to join the church choir, and he just worships Rabbie Burns."

"He's a bit of a mixture. Did ye see any drink?" the two women kept quizzing Evelyn.

"No, but that doesn't say he's not a drinker."

They viewed the man when he appeared again in the hall.

"Tea's at 5.30. Your name's William, isn't it?"

"My name's William, and I don't know what time I'll be back. I service all the fridges in this area: from *Mr Softee*, to butchers' and household fridges, and also the morgue in the hospital."

"What have we done?" Evelyn sat down, wincing at the bang he gave the front door. "The glass'll never stand that."

"Ye'll have to tell him," said Chrissie.

"I don't think he's the kind of man ye tell anything to," Annie said. "That man takes no bidding."

"Rabbie Burns or not," Evelyn said, "he'll toe the line."

Chrissie sat quietly.

"I wonder what vegetables he eats?"

"I never thought to ask him," Evelyn answered, thinking about the dinner.

When tea time came the women found that they wouldn't have any worries about the Fridge Man's appetite or preference for food. He sat at the table, rubbing his hands.

"Hunger's good kitchen," they heard him say as he laid into the bread and butter and jam as well as the salad.

Some of the other boarders were late, and he had swiped all the home baked scones and pastry.

"We've bother here," the women agreed. "Put less out and give each an allotted amount as they come in. It'll be more work but we couldn't hold fit to that gorb. If he drinks the same way we're in real bother."

"He's a tooth picker too, and he flicks the used picks around the fireplace. I'm not stooping to pick those up," Evelyn stated as she washed dishes. "It's bad enough the apple cores stuck with the ashes in the ash tray. How do women put up with men, when they are married and stuck with them?"

The three women shuddered at the habits of men.

The Fridge Man stuck his head around the kitchen door.

"I'll want a bell to my room that you can press down here, as people with broken down fridges phone at all hours for me, and you'll need to tell me. The bell will make it easier for you. Oh, and the firm will be putting in a phone. You have one in the hall already so choose where you want mine to go."

"Wait till Evelyn hears about this." Annie took off her glasses to wipe them and peer at Chrissie. "A *bell* indeed. And we can get pickin' where another phone goes! It won't be to my ear anyway, for I'll never clap one of them things to the side of my head."

Annie's only encounter with their own phone frightened her, and she had held it away from her face and kept shouting to the rest that she couldn't hear anything.

Evelyn appeared and smoothed her hair up at the sides, wetting her fingers to do so. Then she wet the tips of her finger and smoothed her eyebrows. She smiled at herself in the kitchen mirror.

"What's this about a phone?" she asked.

"Another one," Annie said, "and some kind of bell."

"Well, I'll attend to this man. Where did he go?"

They pointed to the dining room.


"A word, please," she nodded to the boarder, who had joined the others in front of the fire, a paper on his lap. He bustled out.

'This one thinks he has authority,' Evelyn thought as she squared herself up.

"This phone and this bell: who authorises it?"

"My firm," was the reply.

"Then who answers it?"

He shuffled about a bit.

"Well whoever's in the hall."

"We just wait in the hall for your calls, then?" Evelyn's eyebrows were now raised and her eyes nearly popped out. "What payment does this person in the hall receive?"

"The firm will let you know."

He disappeared up the stairs and Evelyn joined the others in the kitchen.

"We'll have to change gears for this one, and we're stuck with him."

Then she thought about the dried-up dinners and fries that would be kept in the oven for this man without a timetable.


"Well, we'll see. I hope he doesn't start singing up those stairs. It's enough with the bagpipe player. Would ye ever have thought yon chap was carrying up bagpipes?"

They stopped again to laugh about the way they had watched the owner of the bagpipes – a young chap with big staring eyes and hair stuck up like a badger's – haul his suitcases and bagpipes up their stairs.

He had banged the lot down with each step and Evelyn touched her hand to her head.

"How do we get them? Who reared them?" she muttered to the others.

"Are you playing in a band?" she asked him hopefully, when she got him at the bottom of the stairs.

"Ah no! I have asthma and when I finish work in the bank each day I play to exercise my lungs."

So now they had a musician as well.

# CHAPTER SIX

## Another Business

"Evelyn. There's somebody at the door."

Chrissie and Annie always avoided answering the door as well as the phone. Evelyn always had to hurry from whatever she was doing to attend to these two nuisances.

"I've never a minute," said Evelyn. "Why did we ever agree to that phone for the Fridge Man? I've had enough. Sure weren't you standing at the door. Couldn't you have opened it?"

The muttering was kept up as she made her way down the long hall. A young man stood in the porch, gazing at her with a shy nervous smile.

"You keep boarders. I wonder if you have any vacancies?"

Evelyn took in the fact that the chap was well dressed in country looking clothes, a warm checked shirt and tweed jacket. He was of small build but well set up.

"What do you work at?"

"I'm a vet."

A vet. This was a change from the occupations of the rest of the boarders in the house. 'Apart from a step up in society, he would be a steady payer,' she thought. Maybe she could charge him more. But the rest of them would put him straight about their weekly charge.

"Would you be staying all week?" Her voice now took on a swanky tone as he was a professional man.

"Yes."

"Hold on, excuse me. I'll be a minute."

Evelyn half shut the door , and hurried up the hall to confer with the others. Annie was down in the cellar.

*"He's a vet lookin' board. What'll I do?"* Evelyn whispered down to her.

Annie didn't use a whisper as she bumped the hod of anthracite up each step.

"What do we want with a vet in this house? Haven't we got enough trouble?" asked Annie.

*"Shush!* He'll hear ye."

"I don't care. It's up to you. Look at the bother we have with that Fridge Man. It's up to you," Chrissie kept repeating.

"What's he like?" asked Annie.

"He's another man, like the rest; maybe better pay."

"We'll try him," Annie decided.

Evelyn's polite voice assured the young man that there was a vacancy.

"Could I come pretty soon, like right away?" he asked.

"Well I suppose so."

"I've my luggage in the car."

Evelyn's eyes went to the small box-like vehicle behind him. 'It's bunged to the throat,' she thought.

"I'll show you the room," Evelyn said, allowing the vet to come in from the porch.

They climbed the stairs in silence and he approved the accommodation.

"My stuff will fit in here nicely," said the vet, looking around his lodgings.

They listened as he went up and down carrying cardboard boxes.

"Was that bottles clanking?" Annie's fear of drink in the house was very real. Evelyn went out and stopped him as he hauled up another load.

"No strong drink in there, I hope?"

"None," he assured her. "Just veterinary medicines."

"You'll keep them here?" enquired Evelyn.

"Of course," the vet answered as he struggled with the boxes. "I need them here, as I haven't got any other premises. I'll run my business from here."

Evelyn gazed at his disappearing legs.

'He means it,' she thought. 'This is a nightmare. How will I tell Annie?'

"*Mother*," Evelyn whispered.

Annie was peeling potatoes, her small body sitting in a chair, leaning over a bucket, knees splayed out, elbows resting on the knees.

"Mother, he says he's going to work from here."

"How?" Annie snapped.

"I don't know," Evelyn admitted.

"Ask him, if ye can get him to stop when he goes past ye."

Evelyn rushed out to the hall. Real panic causing her to perspire, as she swiped at dust on a table, an excuse to be standing in her own hall.

"Hold on there," she said to him, and he rested a box on the newel post. "How do you propose to run a business from here?"

"Well," said the vet, "I'll see the animals on the farms, and if they bring them here I'll attend to them in their trailers or cars. Simple."

"How do they contact you?"

"Oh, I'll install a phone. You have space in the hall for it."

It seemed clear cut. Evelyn returned to the kitchen and explained the situation to the others. Annie swung round from the cooker.

"Thought you were complaining about the 'fridge phone'?"

"He'll answer it, he says."

"But when he's out?"

"I never thought," said Evelyn, sitting down. "Now here's a handling. What'll we do?"

"Well he's in now. All we can do is give it a trial."

The vet's phone was installed, and they viewed it and the pad and pencil left beside it. The 'fridge phone' rang. They jumped. Evelyn held the phone away from her ear as she listened to a tirade coming from the other end.

"Some ice cream fridge in a van has packed up. He's fair jumpin' mad. An hour ago it was a woman who had lost all in her freezer. This goes on all day."

Annie viewed the vet's phone.

"It will be good crack when *it* goes as well. These phones all carry nothing but bother down the line, and you'll take the brunt of it."

Evelyn dusted around the handset. 'This one could maybe dance,' she thought.

At 11pm the vet's phone did ring, and ring and ring. The vet didn't hear it. Evelyn rapped on his door as she went down the stairs to answer it.

"It's me sow. It's piggin'," a frantic voice shouted down the line.

"It's Pat Sweeney's pig," Evelyn shouted to the vet as he hurried downstairs.

She left him to go up to the other two standing wide eyed on the landing.

"Will this business keep us from getting our sleep?"

"Not if I can help it," said Evelyn as she got into bed and humped the clothes up around her shoulders. "I didn't think Joe Sweeney kept pigs."

"More fool him."

Chrissie slept in the far corner of the room.

"Evelyn. Was that a knock on the door?"

Evelyn whipped back the clothes, wrapped her old dressing gown around her again and peered out.

The vet stood there, now fully clothed.

"I have to go to this man's sow. I don't know the area. Can you direct me?"

After much wampishing of arms to show the way, Evelyn and Chrissie went down to the kitchen to draw out the directions for this man, concerned that he didn't want to get the wrong people out of bed.

"An' what about us?" the women moaned as they made their way back upstairs again.

Evelyn sat up on the bed.

"I'll have to wait for him. He never asked for a key. Tarnation! That young chap is out the 'morra."

Chrissie went downstairs with her.

"We'll make a cup of tea."


After 1.30am they heard the vet's car stop outside. Then a cheer came from up above. The boarders shouting to the vet from the bedroom windows had heard about the sow's delivery.

"What did she have?" shouted the wee clerk.

"Did she live?" asked another.

Evelyn went to the door, let him in and stood out onto the pavement to yell up to the chaps hanging over the windowsills.

"Get to your beds and keep quiet! The neighbours don't need this."

"Do ye want a cup of tea?" asked Chrissie.

Marshall the vet took off his cap, and sat down to regale them about the night's events. The women were enthralled at descriptions of the birth, the people who were in the piggery – bits of gossip he had heard.

"Take more tea, and here's a soda farl," said Evelyn as she pressed him to tell them all the news.

# CHAPTER SEVEN

## Man or Beast?

"What's that commotion upstairs?"

The usual sounds of banging doors and running water were being interrupted by loud laughter and shouts.

"That's the Fridge Man yellin'," Chrissie told the others, as she listened from the bottom of the stairs. "The folk outside will hear the noise. What's goin' on up there?"

The stillness that descended when the boarders or 'chaps' as Annie called them, knew that the women had heard them, was even more frustrating.

"They're up to somethin'," said Chrissie.

"Go'n up Chrissie, and see what they're at," said Annie.

"Evelyn had better go – she has more authority," her daughter replied.

They didn't like to go up when the chaps were in states of undress. Evelyn climbed slowly, still aware of the silence, and went to the Fridge Man's room. She would tell him about the calls that had been coming in since 7am, as an excuse. Her first tap on his door had no effect, so she knocked loudly and a hoarse voice answered.

"I'm coming in," she called.

The boarders were all around the bed in different stages of undress. Above the smell of their damp towels, toothpaste and aftershave, a heavy odour of sweat filled the air. They moved to let her approach the bed. The Fridge Man lay flat on the mattress, the bedclothes pulled up tight to his stubby chin.

"Where's your pillows?"

One chap pointed to the floor beside the bed.

"What are they doin' there?"

She bent to lift them and heard a whisper from one young boarder.

*"Smother him with them."*

She gave him one of her disdainful looks and viewed the specimen in front of her. She could barely see his face.

"He's not well. We heard him groaning and came in."

"What's wrong with ye, William?" asked Evelyn.

"I'm just a bit under the weather." The voice was a hoarse whisper. His face was hot and mottled looking. "I don't want any breakfast. I just want to lie here, alone."

The boarders tittered.

"It 'd be a good one who'd lie with ye," one of them quipped.

"Now, now, the man's sick. I think I'll get the doctor," said Evelyn.

"No doctor. I'm strong as a horse. No doctor!" He pulled the clothes up tighter under his chin.

Evelyn began to examine the man. His hands were dirty looking – he had just tumbled into bed feeling sick. His sheet where he had been pulling was grubby looking.

"Your bed will have to be changed," Evelyn decided.

"Not necessary." His eyes were shut now. His only escape was to pretend they weren't there.

"You could do with a wash," Evelyn said.

The body under the clothes shuddered at this statement. All eyes turned to Evelyn, waiting on her next move. She reached for the sheet to pull it back. The Fridge Man's hands grappled at the sheet holding it firm.

"He's naked under there," another of the boarders ventured.

"He doesn't wear pyjamas."

Evelyn had to think about the situation.

"I'm sending for the doctor. He's not coming to a dirty bed in this house. Look, have any of you got a dressing gown?"

Nobody would admit to ownership, as they didn't want him to use their clothing.

"Hasn't he got a raincoat? When I go out put it on him. Get him into the warm hot press. I'll put a chair in there for him. Then I'll change the bed."

Evelyn hurried down to get Chrissie to help her change the bed.

"Yon's a handlin' up there," said Evelyn. "He needs a good talking to. When he's better I'll read the Riot Act to him. I'm affronted at the chaps seein' the sight of him."

The two women worked hard stripping the bed, whipping out starched white linen sheets and expertly making it up, smoothing out wrinkles and talking away. They swept up socks and shoes, old jumpers and dirty shirts into their arms, dumping them into the wardrobe.

"Such a carry on. If he blocks that fireplace with any more tissues and sweetie papers, by my sang I'll swing for him."

Evelyn was excited. How would she introduce the doctor to a naked boarder?

They carried the bed linen downstairs and regaled Annie with the situation upstairs.

"You are coddin'," Annie kept saying. "Did you bring down his dungarees? Don't put them in the wardrobe; they're full of oil. Phone the doctor."

Evelyn put on her 'swanky' voice and, holding the phone out from her ear asked for a home visit. No, she didn't know his age or anything about him. A doctor would call.

"How little we do know about any of them living in this house," said Evelyn. "A crowd of strangers."

The kitchen was buzzing with the situation.

"He's in the hot press. The place for him," said Annie.

"What under goodness is going on NOW?" Chrissie wondered. Gouls and yells came from above. "It's comin' from the hot press."

Evelyn and Chrissie rushed upstairs and Annie stood in the hallway viewing the wallpaper and holding onto the newel post.

The boarders were all grouped on the landing outside the hot press. The Fridge Man was still on the chair. A pitiful figure in a wee tight raincoat, roaring like a bull.

"What's goin' on?" the women demanded.

"We thought we could get his temperature taken. He agreed, so we got the vet to get his thermometer, and he brought it down to him. He got him to open his mouth and popped the thermometer in. Then William wised up, and asked where he had last put the thermometer. He said 'John Hamlyn's cow – and it wasn't in its mouth'."

William was whingeing now.

"I'll die, I'll get some infection; the Hoose, or Foot and Mouth. Did you even wipe it?"

A ring at the doorbell changed the scene. All the men disappeared off to the dining room for their breakfast. When they went to work today they had a tale to tell. Evelyn had to face the doctor; Annie had scuttled into the kitchen. The doctor treated William as if he was used to finding patients in a hot press surrounded by sheets and towels, Hoovers and brushes. When he went to open the raincoat, Evelyn went outside. She heard William ask about the diseases that could be got off a thermometer used for cows. She couldn't hear the answers, but she thought the doctor didn't believe him.

"He's got a high temperature, a bout of 'flu," said the doctor.

"Give him plenty of fluids, and he would need to get into bed."

"He'll be looked after, Doctor."

Chrissie saw the doctor to the door and Evelyn escorted William back to his room.

"Why did you sit on in the hot press?" she asked.

"It was warm in there," replied William, the Fridge Man.

"I don't want to see your bed in that state again. Wash yourself or take a bath. Get yourself pyjamas."

As she walked with him Evelyn scolded him, but she could hardly keep from laughing as she watched his wee bandy legs and bare feet scuttle before her.

"I'm happy the way I am," said William

He went into his room and slammed the door.

The women in the kitchen could hardly talk for laughing, at the thought of the thermometer being put into his mouth.

"Don't let him hear ye!" cautioned Evelyn. "Did we get all the oddities in the country to board here? Wait till that vet comes back!"

# CHAPTER EIGHT

## The Spud Man

"Is that somebody at the door?"

The women viewed the shadow through the glass. Another prospective boarder? Annie shuffled up the hall as the other two had not moved. Heaving the door wide open, she came hurrying back to the two in the kitchen. Her eyebrows were raised right up, nearly to her hairline.

"If you see the cut of yon one. He's foreign, with a mouthful of buck teeth, and he's talking about spuds."

Evelyn went to the door. Annie had described him well – he said he was from Malaya, a university student and he needed to stay here to inspect potatoes around the farms. There was something honest about the brown eyes that appealed to her, she told them afterwards, so she told him he could stay.

"This is a quare assortment we have in the house at the present time," Annie remarked.

Annie worked at her baking, making the kitchen table creak and the legs vibrate with her shoving at the pastry mixture. Evelyn showed him to his room, and said he looked so small and thin when he took his coat off. He kept bowing his head to her as she told him about food times. He had hardly any luggage.

"That's always the same," said Evelyn. "The ones from afar travel light, and the local boys carry enough baggage to flit to Africa."

Annie stopped baking to ask about food.

"What'll he eat? We have enough faddy eaters and don't know anything about foreign food."

Now they were beginning to worry. When the brown smiling face appeared at the kitchen door the women jumped – he did have big teeth and he moved so quickly and silently.

"I heard you talking about food," said the new boarder in reply. "Please feed me like the others. I am so grateful that I have got accommodation, as I couldn't get past the door in other places. My main problem will be in finding my way to the list of farms I have here. Their potato crops have to be inspected. Is it all right to park my motorcycle at the front door? I would like to bring it in for safety, but your hall isn't wide enough."

Annie's snort was loud and the table suffered more pounding.

"No, there wouldn't be room in the hall for your motorcycle. It should be happy enough against the wall – not against the window, mind."

Annie knew that like the vet and the Fridge Man, this one would be after her all the time – for directions to places. Especially when she would be busy.

Next morning 'Wan', as they christened him, surprised the women by making his bed and leaving his room spotless. The other boarders watched him as they munched their breakfast. He ate sparingly at fruit he had brought, cutting it up with a small wicked looking sharp knife. Evelyn watched as he ate daintily. Manicured hands deftly cut away at the fruit. He spoke with such a cultured accent and then he was off to examine the spuds. He was 'foreign looking' among the rest of the boarders, but when he went outside and put on his safety helmet, his big teeth were accentuated and he looked really fearsome. His bike roared away and Evelyn laughed with the others, at the impression the potato inspector would have on the local farmers and their wives.

He came back later in the day and left his helmet in the hall.

Evelyn found him gazing into the mirror there.

"Why do all the farm women run away when I drive up their laneways into the yards? Some of them just look at me and slam their doors shut. What is it about me?"

"What could I tell him?" Evelyn said when he had gone to his room. "Those big teeth were a put off for a start, and with the helmet he was like something from outer space. Somebody will report him going around the doors. If we could only find somebody who could go with him. He has to go back twice to each farm."

"What about old Sam?" her sister suggested.

"Now that's an idea!"

Sam visited them every day. A lovely man, he enjoyed cups of tea and home baked scones as he sat beside the cooker. He knew the country farmers and would be ideal as a guide.

"What about him on the back of that motorcycle?" The women laughed and shoved one another around the kitchen at the idea of old Sam on wheels.

Sam was delighted. He borrowed a helmet and was ready next morning for his jaunt to the potato fields. The bike roared away with Sam clutching Wan's small body. Evelyn began to ponder on whether Sam would be insured, but left the thought aside as she began to wonder what to do about the Fridge Man's drinking.

To make potato bread Annie squeezed the hot potatoes through the steel masher, putting all the strength of her arms into the effort. The worm-like pieces landed on the table in a steamy pile.

"He was stovin' with drink when he came in for his tea last night, walking merry legged up the hall. Did you see the cut of him in those oil stained clothes beside that well dressed bank clerk? And his face was as red as fire," said Annie.

"He brought two trout he had caught in some mountain stream, and some wild watercress," commented Chrissie.

"I'd 'watercress' him!" replied Evelyn.

"'Put these in the fridge for my tea tomorrow night,' he says." Annie was cutting the rounds of potato bread before putting them on the griddle. "The snores of him last night were unbearable."

Evelyn stopped in her dish washing and leaned on the sink.

"He has a stomach like a horse. He must have wild dreams. I can't stand the yells of him and the teeth grinding. Do ye think he has nightmares?"

"Then he looks so fresh in the morning. and he lashes into his breakfast," the ladies replied.

The drinking continued and the women were wakened one morning at 2am by the persistent *ring* of the door bell. Somebody was banging on the door as well. Evelyn pulled on her old dressing gown and rushed downstairs. There was no one at the door that she could see. She stepped outside and found a familiar figure propped up against the wall.

"Who left you here?" Evelyn asked crossly. "Get back to where you were drinking."

As he began to slide down, the other two women arrived and stood looking down at the drunken figure.

"What'll we do? We've no need of this. He's out tomorrow," said Annie.

"He's *out* now! How do we get him *in*?" asked Chrissie.

They gazed up and down the empty street.

"Get him under the arms," Evelyn ordered, "and I'll haul on the feet and legs."

"Would he need to go to the lavatory?" Annie quavered.

The other two looked at her in amazement.

"How do you propose we get him to perform?" Chrissie enquired.

"But the bed…" Annie began to whinge, "…the mattress, the carpet."

"Let us get him in first!" Evelyn barked at her. *"He'll pay if he pees."*

The stairs were steep and they hauled and sliped him up to the first landing. Evelyn stood, straightening her sore back, and jumped as the drunk man caught her around the legs, trying to pull himself up by her dressing gown.

"I think a lot of you Evelyn," the Fridge Man mumbled. "You and me could get married."

"Holy Mackerel!" Annie exclaimed, who nearly collapsed beside him. "You've got an admirer here, girl. You could do worse with wild cress and trout, plus you'll always get your fridge fixed."

Evelyn could hardly reach for him again.

"I hate the feel of him, but we have to get him up."

The haul to the next landing nearly beat them, but he was sliped into the room and dumped on top of the bed.

"Should we put him on his side in case he vomits?" asked Chrissie.

At this Annie left the room, muttering "Och, the mattress…"

In the kitchen, after they had washed their hands, 'for you never know where his hands had been', cups of tea were passed around.

"All those men in the house." said Evelyn. "They were bound to hear that narration, and none of them would come to help."

"What did you expect," Chrissie retorted, "when they wouldn't bring a shovel of coal for their fire? Those boys are for nothin'."

Annie kept repeating that she was "too old for this carry on".

"My old bones are all pulled cinery."

Evelyn's back was aching. They were too excited to go upstairs to bed.

"First thing in the morning he's out."

"Will *you* tell him?" One looked at the other.

"Isn't the kitchen odd at this time in the morning?" Chrissie changed the subject. "The fridge sounds so loud, and so does the clock."

"It's because the traffic has stopped," said Evelyn.

The three women sat around the table and listened for any noise from upstairs.

"At least it was a good idea to send Sam out with the 'Spud Man'," Evelyn announced, as she traced crumbs around her cup of tea. "Sam had a whale of time and enjoyed chatting with the farmers and their wives. He even brought back eggs, and one woman has promised him a chicken for Christmas. 'Don Wan' is now grinning from ear to ear."

# CHAPTER NINE

## The Fittings & Gropers

Evelyn liked to look at herself. She was well set up and dressed to advantage. Always tidy and neat, she was the one in the kitchen who could do any kind of rough work and always look 'dressed'. Annie would have flour on the table and have it flying around the kitchen – her face and hair would even have a smattering of it. The sleeves of her jumper were coated and even the dogs were powdered with it. Evelyn rolled out her pastry like a princess and the others marvelled at her tidiness. She wore a well-fitting brassiere. The lady corsetiere who lived near them fitted the three of them every year.

They all stood in the front room, each one stripping off while the corsetiere woman whipped out her tape and went around their bodies, measuring at the appropriate places. They had all washed well before and used plenty of talcum powder.

"Scrub my back Chrissie," said Annie, as she brought a basin into the kitchen and placed it near the cooker while Chrissie helped her.

They used highly perfumed soap to cover any body odour, and new vests were bought for the occasion. This measuring was for garments that had to be made up for them.

Tea would be made and they would settle down to an afternoon of talk and some gossip. The woman went round so many people, and like the hairdressers of years before carried the news of the district around. They found from her how their figures had altered and she would change her merchandise accordingly.

There would be excitement when she arrived some weeks later with her 'boxes of magic'. They were always long boxes, and she would lift out waves of crisp tissue paper before bringing out the items. Stripped again the women would stand to be fitted, watching their images in the mirror above the sideboard. They were pulled in, uplifted and flattened by the garments. They exclaimed about how well they appeared, how pleased they were, and the little woman, flitting about like an eager robin, tweaking and snapping straps as she ran around them, cooed her pleasure.

Evelyn's breasts were a delight to the woman. She said they were the best she had ever fitted, and made her stand sideways to get the full impact of the lift and thrust that the new covering gave them. The room was filled with the smell of perfume, all different essences, from the corsetiere's heavy scent to the various talcum powders the sisters had applied. They were expensive, these pieces of witchery, and after they had expressed their delight the payment had to be made. This was the serious business, and they came into the kitchen to settle the bill.

Evelyn disappeared upstairs to get the cash and counted the money out slowly and carefully, watched by the bra woman, who waited with her white well-manicured hands on her lap until the cash was handed over. Her fingers flashed with sparkling rings – she even wore one on her small finger. Her ruby painted nails drummed on the table, fascinating the women who tried to hide their care worn hands. They could hardly sit down, as the new regalia under their clothing bit into the flesh, nipping here and there with every movement. They had suffered this before and knew that in time this would ease with wear. They also knew that Annie wouldn't suffer this for long. She always loosened the bra part at the back. Leaving it open, it just hung on her.

"What's the point of paying for them if you open them up?"

her daughters asked.

"I just want the heat of them. I'd miss them if I took them off."

Women had to suffer, they agreed. Evelyn always said that when she was uplifted with her new bra, the boarders would come in for their platefuls of dinner and talk to her with their eyes fixed on her cleavage. Annie said that there wasn't any danger with her bra hanging off her back.

They remembered the time the new fangled rubber type corset had come into fashion. A tube shaped thing it was, and Chrissie thought it would save the expense of the corsets. She brought one home and wriggled into it, puffing and gasping as she pulled and hauled it up over her generous thighs. She was in the scullery, and she reached for the tin of custard powder on the shelf behind her. Tipping it into the top of the girdle she found it went on easier. Then she had started to sweat and found movement nearly impossible.

"I'm bluttered!" she kept crying to herself and couldn't leave the scullery to call for help. The others reminded her of how they had found her rolling about in panic. The sweat had made the rubber stick in the custard powder and they finally had to cut her out of the constricting band. The flesh round her middle was covered in red welts where the rubber had tightened.

"My stomach's scalded!" she kept moaning to the others. "I would need the doctor."

"There's no doctor comin' to this house on such a fool errand. How could you explain what happened?" said Evelyn.

Chrissie was sticky with the custard powder, but said she couldn't suffer water to touch her.

"This is some handling," Annie kept muttering to herself, "and on the mouth of tea time. What possessed you to try to get that body of yours into them things?"

The two women viewed Chrissie standing naked in the scullery among the saucepans.

"Keep your head down Chrissie," cautioned Evelyn, "or they'll see you through the top of the window and wonder why you're not coming out. Hand me out those plates and cups before the boarders come in."

Evelyn and Annie began to titter and laugh at the sight of Chrissie, with her head down on the draining board, trying to cover herself with a drying cloth.

"You two won't laugh so much when I tell you how much I have to pay for those roll ons. I only had them out on 'appro'."

All these efforts to enhance the female form seemed to gain the women unwelcome attention. Sometimes Evelyn would come in, lash her messages on the kitchen table and sit down, wiping her face delicately with her lace edged handkerchief.

"He was at it again!"

"Not the day again," Annie would sympathise, making her a cup of tea.

"I only went in for a saucepan and he came up behind me. You wouldn't hear him with those suede shoes he wears. I should have smelled him, with all that greasy muck he put on that frizzy hair of his. He put his arms around me, squeezing my breasts with those big groping hands of his. I flailed about, grasping at the shelf of saucepans and the clatter of them brought yon wee ancient gnome of an office woman out to see what the noise was. He just bent down to pick up the pans and went on as if nothing had happened. I feel dirty. He wrinkled my reveres. The ugly, filthy old brute. Do you think he squeezes her? Is she squeezed done? She thinks the world of him and she thought maybe he was hurt. If I could have got my hands on one of the heavy pans he would have been."

"What's wrong with him?" asked Annie. "Is it the new corset? Does he do this to all the women who buy pans?"

When Evelyn sat in church on Sunday she always watched him step up the aisle with his quiet shy looking wife. When he held the collection plate out to her as he passed it along the pew Evelyn always looked straight up into his face. He would look back, unconcerned. Who would believe he was a groper anyway? It made buying hardware that much harder, but he knew the women had to purchase these goods.

"I'll never understand men," said Evelyn. "We have all the bother with them here, and then I have to fight to buy a pan."

The apple orchard was another place where she had to fight for her honour. The old boy who owned the orchard sent a message to tell them that the apples were ripe and it was time to go for them. Now, the women needed theses apples. They stored them carefully in the old attic and they made their apple pies, apple fool and other concoctions with them. Somebody had to go for them.

"Wear a coat and tie it tightly around you, Evelyn," Chrissie suggested. "Keep looking behind you when you bend down for the fallen ones."

"It's all right for you to give me advice, but I'm the one to face him," Evelyn replied.

It had started when Chrissie had gone with her. They had filled their big baskets with big rosy apples, leaving them for the milk man who said he would bring them in his van. Their baskets had been full and Chrissie, with some kind of devil working in her, had decided to go on picking. She wore big bloomer knickers and had taken off her skirt, climbed onto a branch, and began to shove the apples into her knickers. As she filled them they stuck out in all directions. Evelyn roared with laughter at the sight. The sun shone and they both enjoyed the freedom. Chrissie's laughter rang out, and the old boy who owned the orchard arrived. Chrissie couldn't come down. She had not known that he was near, and he wouldn't leave. He made a lunge for Evelyn and chased her round the old gnarled trees. Chrissie climbed down and got the apples out of her knickers. The milk man arrived and Evelyn appeared gasping, with the old man assuring her that he had better apples further on, strawberries as well.

"That's a quare load of apples and all for nothin'," Annie laughed when they arrived home with their spoils.

The milkman had wondered at the situation these two maiden ladies had been in when he called for them. To avoid gropers was part of life, and each one needed a different strategy. They always wanted to leave on speaking terms.

# CHAPTER TEN

## The Snout

A week always began with the changing of the beds. Each bed was stripped and remarks passed about the occupant. Some beds had the clothes pulled off on to the floor anyway, and the words were sharp as Evelyn and Chrissie had to make their way over them.

"Untidy sods. Look at that pillow case," said Evelyn. "The water must be running out of his mouth all night."

They would then release the clothes at the bottom of the bed.

"Ooh! Smell his feet! How do they stand beside him at his work?" Chrissie wondered.

"Look at his underwear. Jam it all in the drawer," instructed Evelyn.

"He has clean shirts there," Chrissie pointed out.

"Jam them in anyway," Evelyn said. "Why do they stick their socks under the bed, and then we are in a fix when they clog up the Hoover."

Hospital corners were used to tighten the sheets. Freshly starched pillow cases were slipped over feather pillows, and the bedspreads smoothed out. The beds had been attacked by the two women and left pristine with eiderdowns squared on top. They had deliberately turned the bed covers upside down so that the Salvation Army motifs were not noticeable. These women were thrifty and had bought them in the markets. Piles of used bedding were heaped on the landing and taken down to the kitchen in stages. Then the heavy work began. They raked out all items from under the beds. Exclamations and gowls erupted at each discovery of some object.

"He'd six pairs of shoes under that bed, and dirty socks too."

"This boy had golf clubs and tennis rackets under his."

In one room the heavy smell caused them to search for the source. Round and round they went. Heavy foot smells were one thing, but this was more than *heavy*!

"It's like a rotten body," stated Evelyn.

"I've never smelled a rotten body," said Chrissie.

"Well it's like what a rotten body *would* smell like," Evelyn answered. "Did you look under the mattress? My stomach's churnin'…och, it's putrid. Pull the mattress off and we'll slide it downstairs."

"Holy Mackerel what's that?!" Chrissie squealed, as she viewed a blackened mass sticking to the underside of the mattress.

Puffing and panting, the women manoeuvred the bedding down and past Annie in the kitchen. She watched open-mouthed while her relations hauled the big square into the yard.

"It is a skin, but of what? Open the front door," said Annie. "Get a bit of air in here. Make a draught." She changed the subject for a moment. "Did youse remember Mrs Albright said she would call for pastry for the church social? Which wan of them idiots had that in his room?" Annie covered her baking with cloths.

"It's the wildlife chap," Chrissie got out.

"Wait till I get him. I'll teach him about wildlife." Annie started to whinge and ring her hands.

"Mother, quit that. This is bad enough without listening to you. What's to become of us? We're not fit for this."

The phone rang. Evelyn had to wash her hands. The phone stopped.

"This is a carry on."

The phone rang again.

"Who? What?" Evelyn called into the receiver. "Get me paper!" she shouted to the others. "And a pencil." The phone conversation continued as follows (from Evelyn's side, at least):

"What's your name?"

"What's your address?"

"Spell it."

"What's wrong with your fridge?"

"I don't know anything about him."

"Yes, he lives here."

"Report me if you like, sonny."

"I can't help your stuff meltin'."

"He'll get the message."

"That's another handling. They're ringin' up already about fridges. This is getting to be a wile place," said Annie.

"Did the wildlife boy come in yet?" asked Evelyn

"No, but he is due now. There he is," said Chrissie.

Evelyn drew herself up again and stepped slowly up the hall. She surveyed the young man in front of her.

"Come out to the yard."

He followed her and stood facing the mattress.

"What under goodness is it – this skin thing stuck to the material?"

"It's the skin of an otter I caught," he replied, "and I'm trying to flatten it out to roll it up and send it off to get 10 shillings."

The pride in his voice angered Evelyn.

"What about the mattress? It's stained and ruined. You'll have to pay for a new one."

"I haven't the money," the 'wildlife boy' got out. "I was trying for an extra 10 shillings."

He moved to the cellar steps. The women watched him as he went down and fistled behind paint tins.

"Look I've got the snout in here. That should fetch another 10 shillings."

"I wondered what the smell was down there," said Annie. "It's mingin'. It's a wonder we hadn't a plague"

As she sat down she looked out into the hall, at the gleaming black and white tiles. Of late they had wondered at small pockmark holes in the heavy vinyl.

"What have ye got on your feet?"

"My hill climbing boots." He held his foot up with pride. They saw the spikes.

"Get them off ye! Now look at our floor!"

He couldn't see why they were so worked up about it.

"Sure ye wouldn't notice those small holes," he kept saying.

Evelyn gazed between the stinking snout, the mattress and the skin.

"Peel that off and bin it and the snout. You'll lie on it, but I want an amount every week to buy another. And get those boots off or you'll pay for the hall floor as well."

They had to watch him scraping as they prepared the tea.

"My stomach's fair turnin'," Annie kept saying, as she left out the salads on the kitchen table. "Would any bits come in the air onto the food?"

Annie sighed and put plates on the table to start the meal.

# CHAPTER ELEVEN

## The Minister's Visit

"The minister's comin," said Annie. She always got into a tizzy when she heard there was to be a visit. "We'll give the good room an overhaul."

The woman never thought the room was good enough for this elegant man. As well as the usual housework the two big windows were cleaned and polished – Chrissie's arms working like pistons. The curtains were draped 'just so'.

"That cat's been up on the table. Look at the scratch in the surface," said Annie, her face twisting as she worked, keeping up a running commentary as she hurried about. "We're far too particular, but when I sit down I always see dust. Stick the bowl of flowers over that mark. Would he ask to go to the lavatory? Make sure it's clean, and get rid of the boarders' shirts hanging dripping in the bathroom. Put a lock of bleach down the lavatory bowl. He's used to goin' round houses. He'll have gone to the toilet at home. Like the Queen, he'll not ask. We'll take no chances. It might come on him. He's human."

The women worked away but were constantly interrupted by the phone.

"I'm fed up trampin' up and down that hall," said Evelyn. "Every fridge must be broken, and they are shoutin' at me about fish going off – all sorts of damage. I'm takin' the brunt for that firm."

She had washed her hair for this visit and her eyelashes and eyebrows were well covered with Vaseline. She viewed the other two. Annie would wear a long cardigan and a white blouse. She would have to discard the slippers with the big pompoms and wear her sensible shoes. The lisle stockings could be hoisted up tighter on the button used for the purpose. Chrissie would wear a new crossover pinny. As they sat on the sofa Evelyn knew he would see their feet and legs. She always told the other two to keep their knees together and their feet at peace.

Evelyn did have a 'gra', as the others put it, for this particular man of the cloth. He was elegant. His grey suit sat well on him: the round collar was so different from the T-shirts and wrinkled shirts she was used to on the other men. His hands were fine, long fingered and the nails were so well manicured and clean looking. She loved to watch his hands. His silvery hair had a sheen to it, and his eyes were his best feature. When he gazed at her, her thoughts about men changed, and she thought of the peace of his big empty manse. The place had the atmosphere of a church and the smell of lavender polish; it was balm to her soul. For this visit she would get out the china tea set, the plated teapot and the linen tray cloth. All thoughts of otters and snouts left her. *He* would be here, and she could sit and let her thoughts wander. Did he ever look at her, *really* look at her? She had a firm good figure, she thought. Her legs were good. He hadn't a wife. She got so nervous in front of him, almost shy. When she got bogged down with work, Evelyn would daydream about this man. He didn't know that the thought of him kept her sane as she dealt with the men in the house. He was different.

His Reverence liked chocolate cake.

The mixer whizzed and whirred away as Evelyn carefully prepared his favourite cake. It came out of the oven 'as light as air'. The chocolate icing went on top, with her hands shaking in her effort to make a perfect offering to place in front of this man. He wasn't earthy, he was spiritual, she thought as she lit the fire. Scented fir cones filled the room with cinnamon spicy smells.

"That's a wild smell," Annie mumbled to herself. "There's no need for all that. Ye get far too giggited over this visit."

Evelyn waited for the bell to ring, and when it did her heart bounced. There he stood all grey suit, hair and clerical vest. His hand with the long fingers was held out to her. She could hardly breathe, and joined the others on the sofa while he sat back in the big easy chair beside the fire.

'What if the chimney smoked?' Evelyn thought. All her thoughts chorused around 'what if'.

He talked to them about the weather and asked them how they were keeping.

'Please don't let Annie tell him about her bowels,' Evelyn thought.

"We're all very well. And yourself?" Annie asked.

"I'm very busy organising the church social. Will you be able to come?

"I'm not able to attend the meetings any more," Annie told him. "I can't sit for any length of time now," Evelyn held her breath and kept dunting Annie, "but Evelyn tells me all about the sermon when she comes back from church. Ye fairly gave them a trouncing last Sunday, I hear, about 'living in sin'. I'm sure it's not easy to think up new sermons for every week, but there's always plenty of sin for you to preach about."

Evelyn nodded to Chrissie to steer the conversation onto safer ground, while she would go out to make the tea. Evelyn was so relieved that Annie didn't mention her bowels.

'What a man,' she thought as she boiled the kettle for tea in the kitchen. Even the way he spoke sent ripples along Evelyn's spine.

She set the tray with their best cups and linen cloth, and placed it on the coffee table in front of his long legs.

'Look at those shoes!' Evelyn's eyes gazed at highly polished footwear. 'I bet he doesn't keep them gathering fluff under his bed. I wouldn't mind making his bed.' All sorts of thoughts came into her head.

The chocolate cake was lovingly presented. The minister glanced up at the eyes looking intently into his. The long fingers missed their hold on the cup and saucer. The three women watched and listened to the *crack* of the cup hitting the saucer and plate as they crashed to the ground, showering the minister and the lemon coloured carpet with tea. He shot out of the chair, knocking over the chocolate cake.

"I'm scalded, I'm scalded!" he shouted.

The cake landed on the floor at his feet, and the shiny shoes plunged into it as he jumped away from the mess. Those shoes left prints of sticky dark chocolate embedded into the carpet. The front of his immaculate grey trousers was dark with the hot tea.

"Sorry. Sorry," he kept uttering as he made for the door and disappeared out into the street.

The three women gazed at the mess.

"Now what do ye think of 'lover boy'?" Annie asked Evelyn.

Her daughter was on her knees, lifting up pieces of broken china and scraping at the stained carpet with the linen tray cloth. Evelyn didn't answer. The spell with the minister was broken, her dreams shattered. He was just another man, and hadn't the guts to stand his ground. She wanted to get away, to be by herself to get over the shock.

Evelyn really wanted to go to her retreat, the old shed in the back yard. But her mother had to be pacified. Tea had to be made.

Chrissie went upstairs again to do the bathrooms. They could smell the Vim as she attacked the baths, the bleach as the lavatories were scrubbed. They could also hear her swear as she got fanked up in shirts that were drip drying over the bath and hanging on any nails around the walls. She hated having to wipe over the spills from packets of soap powders.

'Why have they got such poor aim?' she thought, when the floors around the lavatories needed attention. The plugholes always held greasy hairs, and the tide marks around the baths made her stomach turn. Chrissie always had to wear warm snow boots and heavy cardigans when she went upstairs, because there was no heating in the upper floors, but as the work got nearer the ground floor she sweated and puffed.

Leaving her Mother with a cup of tea and a promise that she would be back in 15 minutes to wash the carpet and start the food for the boarders, Evelyn headed out to the old shed in the back yard. She had the shed whitewashed. The whiteness almost blinded her when she sat ensconced on the lavatory in the corner. The floor was scrubbed and covered with newspapers. Sometimes she had to twist around on the seat in awkward shapes to catch some piece of news that caught her eye. There was a small painted table next to the lavatory which she used to hold her crossword puzzles, magazines and cups of tea. She would sit on the polished throne, think and relax. It was her haven.

Now that the minister had left she was glad to sit here and think. She had a box of matches and a candle on the table, for the shed had no electricity. At night time the place looked mysterious, exciting. She had hung pictures on the walls, with bits of wood behind them to keep the damp from soaking into their backs. In the corner a big jug held flowers in summer, holly at Christmas and twigs and leaves in the autumn. A big bowl of perfumed *pot pourri* sat on the window sill. Curtains kept prying eyes from peering in at her. Only the bin man came into the yard, but on one never-to-be-forgotten occasion he had opened the door and peered in at her. He nearly collapsed at the sight of her on the lavatory, and at the scream coming from her. He never went in again.

"What's keeping her out there?" Annie quizzed Chrissie. "Isn't there enough to do here? The tea's to be made, and I'm not sure about that Fridge Man."

"Neither am I, but he's here now," said Chrissie. "He's doin' a quare bit of trampin' about up there. He wouldn't put a fire in the old grate, would he? He'd burn us out!"

"He may not, but he'll put everything else in it: sweetie papers, razor blades, used tissues," Annie replied. "Did you put up the notice 'DON'T USE THE GRATE AS A WASTEPAPER BASKET'? Dear knows, but I hate to get down on my knees to pick the stuff out, and the fluff sticks to the bars. I don't know what's worse; that or apple cores in the ashtray."

"I hear her comin' in now. *Don't mention the Minister*," whispered Chrissie. "And it's a good job you didn't mention your bowels either."

The two women laughed as Evelyn came back into the kitchen.

# CHAPTER TWELVE

## Regulettes

Evelyn and Chrissie were getting more and more aware that as the years passed, Annie was dwelling on her bodily functions. In conversation she would pause and ask if they remembered whether she had had a bowel movement on that day. They would look at one another and tell her she had; for if they said they didn't know, Annie would rush to the cupboard and fish out the tin box of Regulettes. Sometimes in her haste she would scrabble at the tiny brown pills and try to count them, to see if she had taken one that morning. Then she would sit down at the kitchen table, the box in front of her, and whinge and whine about how they wouldn't help her.

"Ye don't have sympathy with an old person," moaned Annie. "And what'll I do if my bowels bind up?"

The other two women had to go into the scullery holding on to one another, shaking with laughter.

"Listen to her and that lamenting, If she takes any more her works *will* seize up!"

They always had to have a supply of the tins in the cupboard for fear they would run out.

"They don't make them any more," the young chemist informed Evelyn when she called to top up the tins. This was terrible.

"Are you sure? Have you got any somewhere in stock?"

"No I've sold the last. They were only used by old folk, and they were too strong. Try these milder ones. They are efficient."

Evelyn brought a box of the new tablets home and casually tossed them onto the table.

"There you are, Mother – new laxatives – better than your old ones."

Evelyn knew there would be a reaction, but was not prepared for the crying and wailing from her mother. Since her whole life revolved around her bodily functions, Annie couldn't concentrate on her work.

"What'll I do now?" she kept lamenting.

Annie would sit holding the Regulette box in front of her, counting the last tablets out as if they were gems. She would keep her arms around them in case one would roll off the table and the dog might get it. As they watched her pining for the pills, the two women realised they would have to do something. Annie was getting thinner, as she was eating less, and they knew they were dealing with a serious situation. They asked in the rest of the chemist shops for Regulettes, but always got the same answer: 'We don't stock them any more'.

Annie would look at them expectantly when they arrived back having ventured further a field in their important quest.

"Have they got any?"

"No luck, Mother."

"Try the others."

Evelyn would tell Chrissie it would have been better for Annie to have been hooked on drink or drugs than Regulettes.

Evelyn was visiting a sick friend in Ballycastle, and called into a chemist to buy soap and talc for a present.

"You wouldn't happen to have Regulettes?" she whispered.

"Oh yes," the chemist replied. She watched him slap the magic tin down on the counter.

"Could I have some more?" asked Evelyn, her face all lit up.

"Of course. How many boxes do you want?"

"Give me seven, please."

Evelyn was nearly purring, as she watched him place seven more tins on the polished surface of the counter.

"Come far?" The chemist talked on as he took the money and regarded her.

She felt so happy, and she knew her face was all lit up as she handled the parcel. She stood outside the shop and talked to herself.

"I need to buy more, but he'll think I'm mad. I'd better get more."

She walked back in.

"Give me fifteen more boxes, please," Evelyn said.

This time the chemist was quiet. The transaction was carried out in silence. Evelyn could hardly wait to get home.

The other two were busy preparing the tea when she got back. When she left down her parcels and took her coat off, she kept the bag containing twenty-two tins of Regulettes until Annie sat down at the table. With a flourish that would have done a magician proud, Evelyn splattered the tin boxes before her. The old work-worn hands lifted the laxatives and caressed the square boxes.

"I'd rather get these that £1000," Annie kept saying.

Now Chrissie took over.

"These will have to be kept carefully somewhere, Evelyn. If she goes at them because there are so many she will run the guts out of herself. We'll have to ration them. As long as she knows we have them, she'll be OK. And listen, Annie. On no account tell those boarders that you have got these, or mention 'bowels' to anybody!"

The kitchen was a place without tension now, and they could

concentrate on their boarders, 'the chaps' as Annie called them. The problem of Annie's bowels had been put to rest, for the time being at least.

# CHAPTER THIRTEEN

## The Cowlodger

Chrissie always wanted to brush the footpath in front of the house in the mornings. It was a form of escape for her to get outside. She would tidy her hair a bit in the hall mirror, straighten her cardigan, pick up a brush and head for the door. Once her head was down ("concentrating on the cement," she said) she felt happy. The brush was expertly twisted and turned in her hands. The small stones were shoved sharply into a pile as she walked around, attacking them from all sides. This pile was carefully shunted into a shovel and carried across the road to a hedge, where it was thrown over. It made her feel good, she told the others. She felt angry when sweet wrappers and chip paper bags in her path, which forced her to mutter away to herself.

"If I caught them I'd wring their necks. There's enough work inside the house clearing up without this extra."

She would glare at the young ones passing by.

"They ought to have bins strapped to their backs," she would mutter to herself, "the amount of empty Coke bottles and chewing gum they need to throw away."

Chrissie liked a chat with people who stopped with her. 'Grand day' and 'How are ye?' would start off a conversation that would eventually yield some newsy titbit to take in to the others. Her eyes would gleam as she listened, and she would question the speaker, covering the news from every angle so that she could tell the complete story herself. Then the brush would come into play again. The soft dust needed to be swept in small movements to clear the pavement and the pile again carried to the hedge. Chrissie just stepped onto the road carrying the dust pan in front of her and forgot to look for traffic. Horns would blow angrily at her, but she just kept on her journey to the hedge.

"Some of these days you'll be hit," Evelyn would tell her.

"No fear," she would reply. "If they don't see me they shouldn't be driving."

This cleaning procedure was necessary, otherwise the debris would be blown into the porch and tramped into the house by the boarders. The women had bother trying to get them to wipe their feet. The porch and the hallway were 'the mouth of the house', Chrissie would tell the other two.

"It tells how the rest of the house is kept," she would say.

On one occasion Chrissie left her tools outside and decided to get the chamois to wipe the window at the front of the house. She wet the cloth at the sink and began to tell her sister about somebody who had died suddenly.

"What's that commotion in the hall?"

Annie got up from peeling potatoes and opened the kitchen door.

"Holy Mackerel! A cow's in the hall, a cow's in the hall!"

The women stood gaping at the big animal. Its body was wedged between the wall and the staircase, and there it stood snorting mucus from big wide nostrils. Eyes madly rolling, the big body tried to push and heave on through the hall.

"Och, the lovely wallpaper, look at the cut of it," lamented Annie. "What it hasn't slabbered on it's shaved off."

Annie ran up to the animal and reached for an umbrella off the stand.

"Don't poke it to make it worse," Evelyn began, taking command. "If we could shove it back..." She ran and got a sheet from the line, and told the other two that she would climb over the stair handrail and get the sheet around the cow's neck. Then she would use it like a lead, and pull while they could push. Evelyn got up on a stool and found it hard to get over the sloping handrail.

"Isn't this a handlin'!" Annie kept up a whine.

The cow began to *moo*, and Evelyn said she didn't know which was worse – Annie's moans or the cow's noise. She had difficulty getting her leg high enough.

"That's some shape if anybody sees ye!" Annie was scared that Evelyn could break a leg – or worse.

"Who's to see me? There's never a boarder when you would be glad of one. Who owns this cow anyway? You'd think somebody would miss it! Chrissie, it's your fault for leavin' the door open."

"I'm always blamed. Did I know a cow would drop in? Aw look, it's wet itself."

The noise of the splashing water galvanised Evelyn into shoving her body after her leg. She leaned over the cow, trying to get the sheet like a rope over the animal's head.

"If I fall over, I'll be on its back."

"Maybe ye could ride it out backwards," Chrissie giggled.

When the sheet was around the cow's neck, Evelyn tried to haul it backwards, with the other two women shoving from the front.

"My stomach's turning with its breath," said Evelyn, "and the runs sparkin' from its nose. This is hopeless. If only Andy would come."

"What would old Andy do?" asked Annie.

Chrissie lay back against the wall, giggling again.

"Not much except ask how he was goin' to get his tea, and 'What's that big cow doing in the hall?'"

Annie couldn't push any more.

"I'm doin' my insides no good with this carry on."

"Go you in and sit down, Mother."

Evelyn decided to go into the street. She could get out now from the stairs, but what would she say to any men she might meet?

"Just tell them we've a cow in the hall, jammed right in the hall," said Chrissie, now laughing till the tears were streaming down her face. "An' me out cleanin' up that pavement to keep the hall tidy."

"Should we phone the Police, or the Fire Brigade?"

"Get them both," Annie shouted from the kitchen. "If it stands long enough it'll wet again. The hall's swimming as it is. I can see it nearly up to the kitchen door. It'll seep under that linoleum stuff and cause a right smell."

"Mother. Don't go on and on about it."

"This is a pickle." Chrissie's feet were wet now and she didn't laugh. "Don't let the boarders walk through that and go upstairs. They can stand in the porch. There they are." Chrissie greeted the men who came into the hallway. "Don't you dare mishandle this cow or beat it. Put that stick down."

One young lively man leapt upstairs and landed down beside her. He started to push the cow with his hands and leaned his full weight on it. It began to go backwards. It seemed to know he was helping, and gradually it was near the door. The young fellow was talking away to it. The beast was sweating and wild eyed, but wanted out. He manoeuvred it through the doorway and onto the pavement. Passers-by stopped in amazement to see the big bulky animal step out and turn to walk up the street.

"Was it looking for lodging?" a girl laughed to her companion. "They feed well in that house: fresh meat on the hoof!"

The women were shocked at the episode.

"It doesn't come in on ye till later," Annie announced as they surveyed the mess. "My body's all shook up, haulin' and shovin' at that cow."

"We can't make tea till it's cleaned up."

Chrissie got the mop and bucket out and work began. Annie worked at the food. The floor was washed and dried. Evelyn ran her fingers over the wall paper.

"Two rolls will fix this. The poor cow would neither lead nor drive."

A boarder came in and stopped inside the door.

"What's that smell?"

"Och, we had a visitor. A cow came for lodgings."

He didn't believe them and went upstairs, watching the women over the banisters. They just seemed to be cleaning as usual. It was such an odd smell.

# CHAPTER FOURTEEN

## 'Something Inwardly'

Annie didn't feel too well following the 'cow episode'. She had shoved and pushed at the animal and she told the others that something had 'given' inwardly. When they mentioned a visit to the doctor, she rushed about and wouldn't talk about it. The other two talked it over in loud whispers, both deciding that on account of her age she should see a doctor for a complete check up. They had to try to talk her round to the idea.

They decided on a strategy.

"We'll keep telling her how pale she is, and that she's slowing up for a start."

Evelyn used the phone to make a call for an appointment and didn't tell Annie. She would tell her nearer the time, but the appointment was in two days' time.

'I'll have to get her to take a bath,' she thought.

Annie was always spotless, washing herself at night in the scullery, but this called for the 'big wash'. Annie noticed the way they were persuading her to bathe, and it dawned on her that they were working up to a doctor visit.

"I'm not goin'! Ye can't make me."

She rushed around the kitchen slamming cupboard doors and making cries of despair.

"Don't let them hear you, Mother. It's for your own good."

"I'm not like a car. I don't need an overhaul. I only hurt myself shoving that cow. Anybody's insides would be shook up with that.

I'm tellin' ye I'm not goin' to that place."

They wore her down and finally got her to the bathroom. The water was frothy and warm. Her leg would not lift high enough to go over the edge of the bath.

"Get a stool and we'll lever her up."

The two women were sweating with their efforts, and they wanted to get the job done before the boarders came back. Annie kept up a kind of *weenying* sound, and told them that she couldn't see.

"It's the steam on your glasses, Mother. Take them off."

"No way. I need to see what you're doin' with me," protested Annie. "Is the water too hot? I'll break my legs. This is cruelty. I'm old: I'm not fit for this."

"Lift your leg up now Mother. There, you're in now. Sit down."

They viewed the figure in front of them. Annie had never been seen naked, and her back view was reflected in a mirror.

"You've put on a quare bit of weight."

"I'm not here to be judged. You've a neck on ye, the pair of ye. If I sit down, I'll never get up."

"We'll lever you down. Ease yourself lower."

Annie hit the water with a splash, and groped for the sides of the bath.

"That didn't help whatever is wrong with me inwardly."

Both women got face cloths and a big bar of rose perfumed soap and fell to the washing. Evelyn's hair worked its way out of her bun and straggled around her face. She was on her knees, working away. Annie just sat stiffly, letting them lift her arms and move her body as they wanted. Her small round glasses slipped to the end of her nose.

"No hair-washing mind. *This* is enough for wan day."

They had to get her up and out. The bath mat gave some

stability, but the both of them had to clasp her slippery body and lift her full weight. Annie's legs just shuffled about uselessly, so they heaved and pulled, gripping her under her arms.

"It's nearly as bad as the cow," Chrissie muttered. This was the wrong thing to say in front of Annie.

"Right. I'll sit here," she announced as she planted herself back firmly on the mat. The steam was running down the bathroom walls and the women were bathed in sweat.

"Open that bathroom window wide, Chrissie," Evelyn shouted.

"No! the cold will kill me!" Annie started to cry. "This is a handlin'. Is there some place to report about cruelty to old people?"

Finally they got her out unto a chair.

"Never again!" Evelyn gasped as she helped dry Annie off.

"You can say that again!" Annie complained.

She never tried to help them. She kept her arms down to her sides, making them really work over her body.

"That towel's too rough. It's scratching me. Be sure to dry between me toes. I don't want that Althletic Foot."

The two women toiled away over the irate body. Chrissie reached for rose perfumed talcum powder and shook it over Annie's back. Annie spluttered and coughed as the white powder came up round her.

"Now you've choked me with that awful dust. That's bad for a body's lungs."

"We want you clean and fresh. We've enough work in the house without havin' to bath you," Evelyn told her.

"You brought it on yourselves. What do I want with a doctor? All my innards are loose and coming down. It's only natural, and this haulin' about didnae help them. I look like a plucked chicken." Annie had caught sight of herself in the mirror. "How under goodness do people bath every day. It'll be a while before I get in there again."

Evelyn pulled a thermal vest over Annie's head. and got her dressed, without any help from Annie.

After this episode there wasn't much talk in the kitchen, from then until the appointment. Annie was dressed in her best clothes and insisted on wearing her hat and gloves.

"Nobody wears hats and gloves now," Chrissie told her.

"Well I do!" said Annie. "And when we are in the waiting room you're not to tell the other folk what I'm going in for. Nobody's business but mine."

"Well, when you talk about your bowels to everybody, I didn't think you cared."

"Will I tell the doctor about them?"

"Whatever you like. But don't say you got fifteen boxes of Regulettes."

The waiting room was busy, and men got up and gave their seats to Evelyn and her mother. Annie now sat like a queen, and nodded to right and left. She had never been to a doctor before and didn't know how to act, except that to her this was an occasion. Some people came over to shake hands. They hadn't seen her for years, and she held court smiling, and looking so gracious, that Evelyn found it hard to believe this was the same woman who had sat in the bath earlier. Evelyn stared at the wall. She was exhausted, and began to think she herself needed an examination.

Annie shook the doctor's hand and settled herself in the chair beside his desk while he shuffled his papers and examined her card.

"If all my patients were as healthy as you," said the doctor, "I'd not have a practice. You've never been here before. What can I do for you?"

"Nothing!" Annie practically snapped. "It's these wans here

think I should come."

"Doctor," said Evelyn, "we had a cow jammed in our hallway and my Mother did a good bit of shoving and pushing to get it out, and she said something snapped inside her."

"Where did you feel the snap?"

"Inwardly, Doctor, but it's of no importance."

"I'd like to examine you."

He swung a curtain around a couch and Evelyn guided Annie behind it.

"I'm not getting looked at." Annie's back was up again. "I'll take my hat off, but that's as far as it goes. I had enough getting a bath."

The doctor took her pulse and blood pressure, but couldn't get her to lie down on the examining table. He referred her to a 'g-clinic'.

When they arrived home Evelyn needed the cup of strong tea Chrissie had prepared for them.

"I never was as affronted as in that room. There she sat, her hat on her knee and she wouldn't budge. Well, you'll have to go to the other clinic, Mother, in two weeks' time."

"We'll see," Annie replied as she dipped a ginger snap into her cup. "It's all a lot of rot. I'm old, wearin' out and nobody'll change that. Nobody's goin to prod around me."

The 'g-clinic' had a waiting room, and Evelyn joined her mother and a group of very nervous women. None of the eight patients spoke at this clinic. They watched the door where the consultant had gone in to start work. A Sister who had a rounded chest and bottom bustled in. Her red uniform made her look like a robin, and her bottom stuck out, making the open V of the white apron wider at the back. She plodded across the room on big flat feet and turned to address the women.

"Now get off your skirts, girdles, corsets and knickers and tights. Put them on your knees."

She saw disbelief on the nervous faces in front of her. Nobody moved. Evelyn noted that she hadn't mentioned hats.

"Come on now," the Sister chivvied them. "You're all women together."

A woman nearest the door began to strip. She was a big country woman, and her face was bright red. It was so red it looked sore, Evelyn thought. Her neck was scalding red. She hardly had space to turn, and she began to peel her skirt down. All eyes turned to watch her. She had no petticoat, and she wrestled with corsets that bit into her armpits and under her breasts as she twisted and turned to unlace them. The long interlock knickers – 'Directoire', Evelyn named them in her head – were caught under these corsets. Eyes were closed as the woman got up to completely divest herself of the rest. The sweat smell was now heavy in the room.

The next woman began to strip at a nod from the Sister. Answering a barking voice from behind the door, clutching her clothing, the big woman disappeared, her red jumper still on top and the big bare buttocks, hips and legs moving quickly. The doctor's voice made them jump. He might have been in the room. The woman was being asked intimate personal questions and they could hardly hear her answers.

"Come on now girls, hurry up."

Evelyn listened to the Sister and glanced at Annie, who sat, hat still on and gloved hands clasping her big black handbag. She watched Annie get up, begin to move.

'She's going to strip,' she thought, but Annie's body was facing the other door, the one that opened onto the way out. With deliberate slow steps Annie walked past the astonished Sister. She nodded pleasantly to her, opened the door and left the room.

"Nobody's goin' to listen to me talk about my body, especially my bowels," said Annie, affronted. "Did ye ever see the like of that carry on? No wonder I never frequented doctors."

When Evelyn got Annie home she could hardly tell Chrissie about the episode for laughing. As she slapped the table between bouts of giggling, Evelyn said she couldn't get over the corsets and the whole procedure. Annie still sat with her hat on, viewing the two of them.

"I'm sufferin' from delayed shock," she told them. "Keep a body from illness and doctors. Thank goodness we don't need doctors here."

# CHAPTER FIFTEEN

## Houd

Annie's eyesight had always been weak, and her two daughters were greatly amused at the way she peered into things. She would hold vegetables up to the light, to ascertain whether she was scraping a carrot or a parsnip. Her eyes would be squinting at the work in her hands, and the daughters feared for her fingers as she flashed the sharp vegetable knife about.

While Evelyn and Chrissie were shopping one Saturday morning, Annie's old friend Lizzie McMurty called and left her a pile of scallions. While the daughters were out Annie decided to make the dinner for them – a surprise dinner. She would make 'houd', the old recipe that they all loved.

There was only old Andy and the Fridge Man for the weekend, so a meatless dinner would suffice. She put the potatoes on to boil and began to chop the scallions into fine pieces. Soon the kitchen began to fill with the earthy smell of boiling potatoes. She stuck a knife into one to test if it was ready, and then poured the boiling liquid into the old stone sink. The potatoes now had to be pounded with the masher, and then worked to a cream with butter and milk, before being laced with the scallions.

Chrissie and Evelyn arrived and surveyed the feast being prepared for them.

"Old Andy won't be here – he is out with his nephew. But the Fridge Man is waiting in the dining room." Evelyn dolloped a mound of the creamy mixture onto a plate, made a well in the centre of it and filled the hole with butter. "Fit for a king," she murmured as she carried it through.

The Fridge Man threw down his paper and viewed the plate.

"I'd rather have that than all your steaks," he told her, as he began to spoon the mixture into the butter.

"He was nearly eating the plate!" Evelyn told the others, as they sat down to their food. "He's sleeping in front of the fire and won't move till night time."

Annie just ate toast. She said the scallions would give her heartburn. The women could relax for a while and just sit and talk, easing their legs and feet and planning the week ahead.

The door burst open and the distraught figure of Lizzie McMurty rushed up the hall and confronted them.

"Ye didn't use those leaves I gave ye Annie?! They weren't scallions. They were daffodil leaves. I got them mixed up!"

Evelyn and Chrissie got to their feet, and all eyes were on Annie. Her thick fingers hovered over some crumbs on the edge of the table and swept them into the palm of her hand.

"I made houd with the leaves," she got out, not looking up.

Evelyn's hand shot out.

"You've poisoned us!" she cried, pointing at her mother. "Holy Mackerel! Did you not look at them? Did you not smell them, when you chopped them?"

At each question Evelyn's voice went up into a squeal.

"How do we stand?" Chrissie pleaded. "We haven't made a will. Mother, *you* didn't eat any. You'll be left on your own."

Annie looked worried at this. The thought of, as she put it 'a wheen of daffodil leaves' didn't register with her as serious, but the idea of being left by herself with all the work did waken her up to the situation. They heard a movement in the hall, feet rushing upstairs. Then the sound of loud retching could be heard from the bathroom. They had forgotten about the weekend boarders.

"He's sick already; he ate a quare melder of that houd." Chrissie was rubbing her stomach and holding her head. "I feel sick, my stomach's burnin'."

Chrissie rushed along the hall to the cloak room. Her retching could be heard joining with the upstairs noise. Evelyn went out into the old lavatory in the yard. Annie sat shocked, gazing at Lizzie McMurty.

"*What'll we do?*" Annie whispered.

"Phone the doctor," Lizzie told her.

"I can't use the phone. You do it."

"I'm not much good at phones either. Where is it?"

"There are two in the hall. Use the one nearest ye," Annie directed.

"What's the number?"

"Look the book."

"What book?"

"It's hangin' up above the phone. The number's beside 'Doctor'," Annie explained.

"What'll I say?"

"Say people are sick: they ate daffodil leaves. Don't say you gave them to me, and don't say I cooked them!" Annie shouted out to her. "This is a quare handlin'."

"I've got through," said Lizzie, who then put on a bit of an accent. "This is from the Tracey house I'm speakin'. Is the doctor there?"

"He's not in yet," Lizzie relayed to Annie.

"Ask her about daffodil leaves…"

"She says she doesn't know," Lizzie replied. "They always meant to get a book on poisons, but haven't got one."

"Put the phone down," Annie called. "There's no help comin' from there."

"Would they need drinks of water, or maybe a cinnamon sweet? To taste their mouths," said Lizzie.

"Don't be daft Lizzie, they can't keep anything down. Do ye not hear them? The place could be in a wild mess. What'll we do? Go out and ask Evelyn in the yard. Shout through the door at her."

"I don't like to intrude!" Lizzie was scared.

"Go on, somebody has to take charge." Annie sat listening to the noises in the house. She told Lizzie to phone the doctor again.

"He's still not in."

"Put the phone down and bring that book in to me." Annie peered over the pages, until she came to the letter 'V'.

"I'm lookin' for 'V'," she told Lizzie. "There he is – get this number on the phone."

"But a vet?" Lizzie looked at her in astonishment.

"Aye, he's a vet, and he knows more than a doctor. And forby ye'll get to talk to him at all times, not like the doctor's!"

Lizzie got the number and shouted back to Annie. "He's here! Will I tell him what happened?"

"Tell him, and ask him what to do."

"He's Scottish, and hard to follow."

"Listen harder then," said Annie.

"He says daffodil leaves are 'toxic', whatever that is, and the coos'll not even eat them. Yer to get the eaters to the hospital."

"The hospital!" Annie moaned. "Not the hospital. They're goin' to die right enough." Annie hauled herself up and went out to the lavatory in the yard.

"Ye're to get the rest to hospital, Evelyn. Now!" She yelled upstairs to the Fridge Man. "Come down! Ye're for the hospital."

A sorry crew arrived in the hall, pale faced and bent over. Evelyn got her car keys and they filed out. They clambered into the car, holding their stomachs all the while.

"You can't go, Lizzie. Stay with me," said Annie.

"What if they need the lavatory on the way?"

"Don't talk about that, Lizzie. Just make me a cup of strong tea."

The sick people made their way into the hospital where they were met by an Indian doctor.

"What is wrong?" Other patients were watching, interested in their answers.

"Well we ate daffodil leaves," replied Evelyn.

The doctor started to speak, astonished at this reply, and Evelyn told him about the cream potatoes, the butter in the middle, the scallions.

"Why did you use daffodil leaves, and what are 'scallions'?"

Evelyn got 'spring onions' out between tight lips. The Fridge Man disappeared, and Chrissie found him lying in the lavatory floor at the entrance. He had left the door open.

"The people will see ye."

"I don't want to die alone," the Fridge Man moaned.

"Neither do I," she told him, and rushed back to the rest.

They sat before a big arrangement of *daffodils*.

"Keep swallowing and breathe deeply," Evelyn told Chrissie.

The doctor was away for some time, and came back to inform the group that he had been on to the Royal Hospital. They had been poisoned and needed to have their stomachs washed out.

"That won't be necessary," Evelyn said. "We seem to have got rid of the worst of it."

"What about the male patient?" asked the doctor, as he viewed the figure on the floor. "I need to wash out your stomach."

"Not on your life!" The sick man raised himself up, holding onto the lavatory seat. "I'm off!" He staggered outside.

Evelyn and Chrissie got to their feet trying to look dignified.

"*Such an advertisement for our boarding house,*" Evelyn whispered to Chrissie. "Feedin' them daffodil leaves. It'll be round the town – that Lizzie McMurty will see to that. And the folk in the church will hear about it. How can I hold my head up as I walk up the aisle?"

"Keep walking now, till we get out of here." Chrissie wanted home.

A nurse came out and informed them that daffodil leaves made you sexy! They viewed the grizzled head of the Fridge Man standing at the door, and began to laugh. At home Annie sat beside the cooker.

"All that fuss about nothing. It was all in yer minds."

"Do you think so?" Evelyn eyed her as she eased herself into a chair. "How come the doctor has officially recorded you as 'the poisoner'. It goes to the Royal, and you Lizzie, as her accomplice. You are lucky the Police weren't called."

Annie clutched her heart.

"If ye had cut up a daffodil bulb and we had eaten it, we would have died. They're lethal."

Lizzie had moved to the door to quietly disappear, but Annie knew she would not be free from their wrath for some time to come. Taking a cup of tea to the Fridge Man, she viewed him as he sat staring into the fire.

"The stuffing's knocked out of him," Evelyn told them later.

"He left most of it in the bathroom upstairs," Chrissie announced.

"I thought I was going to die," he kept saying. "I could see myself in thon fridge where they keep the stiffs in hospital. The one that I have to service."

Evelyn threw more logs on the fire. What could she say to him?

The drink that he consumed never had the impact on him that the daffodil leaves had.

# CHAPTER SIXTEEN

## Miss Lucas

The door bell rang. The strident sound never failed to make the women jump. How they hated these interruptions.

"That door bell has never stopped the day," said Evelyn, wiping the beads of sweat from her upper lip. The kitchen was so hot with the steam from the saucepans bubbling on the cooker. She patted her hair down as she peered into the small hall mirror, before opening the front door. As she told the others afterwards, the smell of perfume nearly overpowered her when she opened the door. A tall fair-haired woman stood on the step.

"Have you any vacancies? I need to stay for two nights." The glamorous figure waited for a reply.

"Hold on a minute." Evelyn walked down the hall and into the kitchen. This wasn't a decision she could make on her own. They had never entertained a female before, but there was a room vacant.

"Take her," said Annie. "It's only two nights, but charge higher money for the change of bed linen."

The new boarder swept into the hall and up the stairs in front of Evelyn. With each swish of her wide skirts the heavy perfume was wafted back, filling the hallway.

"You have the use of the bathroom at the end of the corridor," Evelyn informed her. "And don't hog it for too long in the morning, as the chaps need to get to work."

Evelyn descended slowly. Were they wise taking a woman among all the men?

"I never saw so much lipstick on one mouth," she announced to the others in the kitchen. "Her name is Miss Lucas, and she is coming to lecture on the art of make up."

The three women began to laugh as they looked at one another.

"Do ye think we need help in that direction?" asked Chrissie. "Wait till the men smell her in the house."

The usual noise of chairs scraping back and knives and forks clattering on the plates at tea time stopped, when Miss Lucas put her head around the dining room door.

"Am I in the right room? I could smell the salad from upstairs."

Some of the men stood up, the rest sat and gawped at this vision in front of them. She sat down beside the Fridge Man, and her scent mingled with the oil on his clothes. They all passed bread, salt and salad cream up beside her.

"If you could see yon pantomime," Evelyn told the others in the kitchen. "They are actually pouring out the tea for her. These are the boys we always said were paralysed, when they came through that front door and wouldn't lift a finger to help themselves. I actually saw Jimmy clodding on peats and asking her if she was warm enough. They are laughing and talking, and not the same chaps at all."

The women sat over their tea and wondered at this change in the menfolk.

Chrissie met the woman on the landing later that night, and viewed Miss Lucas' apparel in wonder. The bright purple nightdress was held up by two thin straps, big breasts on display, the shiny satin material shimmering as she moved. Chrissie wanted to cover her up. She wanted to reach into the hot press and get a blanket out to throw over her shoulders. Her shoulders were so soft, and so shiny looking. She carried a big white bath towel and a large bottle of bath salts. 'We'll never sleep with all this smell,' Chrissie thought as she made her way to the bedroom.

"Would any of them try to break into her?" she mused, as she described the nightdress to the others. "There's no lock on the door."

"None of our men would face that woman," Annie figured.

"They might surprise you. They're men after all," Evelyn said. "We'll listen to see if we hear her door open again. That door has a squeak and the floor board outside the door is loose too."

"Will we take it in turns to listen?" asked Annie. "How'll we know if she's only going to the toilet? It was bad enough keeping awake on account of the Fridge Man. Now we'll lose our sleep over this fancy woman."

"This could get us a bad name," Chrissie piped up as she took off her vest. "Maybe we shouldn't have taken her in. If you could have seen the cut of her on that landing!"

"Maybe we should have given her an extra hot water bottle," Annie added.

The men were all seated in the morning when Miss Lucas came down for breakfast. Her chair was pulled out and she was given the same treatment as before.

"You can see the thick make up in the daylight," Evelyn announced as she finished serving Miss Lucas' breakfast order. "She wants fresh squeezed orange juice and crisp toast. The lipstick is thick on the lip of the cup already."

Breakfast over, Miss Lucas appeared at the kitchen door.

"Would you ladies like a make up session?"

The three worn faces gazed at this woman who looked to them like a different species. In her high heels she towered over them. Her colourful clothes lit up the old kitchen. Her scent filled the air. They giggled and one looked at the other.

"Well," Evelyn spoke up unexpectedly, "I'll have a wee bit of time, and there's nobody about."

As Miss Lucas went to collect her tools of the trade, Annie started on Evelyn.

"Are ye wise enough – a face do at your age. Have a titter of wit."

"Look it's only a bit of crack. Give me peace."

When Miss Lucas came back, she settled Evelyn in a kitchen chair and put a pink bib around her shoulders. Evelyn's face was flushed with excitement. She lay back as instructed, and closed her eyes tightly. Her face was lathered with cleansing cream and then a face mask was smoothed on, and she was left while it thickened. Then Chrissie decided to get her face cleansed.

Annie stumped about the kitchen, slamming down pots and pans and rattling dishes as she washed the breakfast things. She kept muttering to herself that these two were far too giggited, and made excuses to make them shift as she passed them. The hall door opened and the bread man carried in his goods on a tray. He looked at the scene in the kitchen – two women were now sitting with white plastered faces.

"Everybody well?" he asked.

"All's fine," Evelyn got out between stiff lips. "See you tomorrow."

"What'll he think?" Annie said. " I thought yese had more sense. I've got through till now with soap and water."

The two women washed the masks off over the kitchen sink, and noted that their skin was fresher and pinker already. Foundation was smoothed on, and powder applied with a big brush. Miss Lucas moved deftly around her two clients, flicking blusher onto the cheeks, chins and brows. When the coloured eyeshadow was brushed on Annie couldn't stand any more, and left the kitchen. She could be heard raking out the fire in the dining room, passing them with the pan of ashes. She puffed hard as she passed them, to emphasise she was carrying on with the chores. She was just in time, as she walked back, to see lipstick being painted on with brushes. Eyebrows were darkened and smoothed. They were told to bite on tissues to set the lipstick, and then Miss Lucas began on their hair. Using yet another brush, their hair was teased out and back combed.

"To give fullness and height," she explained.

Annie was ready to explode.

"I'm making tea, if any of you could sip it," she told them.

Annie never looked at their faces. The two women got up a bit unsteadily and made for the mirror in the hall. They turned their heads this way and that. Putting on the overhead light, they peered in again. The faces that looked back at them were so colourful – not like their faces at all. Miss Lucas gazed in beside them.

"What do you think?" she asked.

"It's not bad! I'm younger lookin'," Evelyn said.

"Wash it off," Annie told them. "Don't let the chaps see your faces. Yer like street women."

She bustled about with the dinner, looking over her shoulder, her small mouth tight, brows drawn together with disapproval. Miss Lucas, who had been faced with more opposition than Annie in her lifetime, approached her with a pot of cream and tried to advise her on how to get rid of her wrinkles.

"It's the work of the Devil you're at," Annie spat at her. "It would fit you better if you'd all worry more about your souls."

There was no answer to this, and Miss Lucas gathered up her tools and disappeared.

# CHAPTER SEVENTEEN

## Sister woman Carmel

Evelyn usually bought linens from a man who had a stall on Fridays in the main street. He had pieces of linen, surplus pieces from a factory somewhere, and these made luxurious sheets for the boarding house beds. Pillow cases in the finer linen were more expensive but well worth the extra. These items were taken home, lovingly examined and then boiled and starched. Evelyn made the starch from cornflour, leaving a firm but silky finish. She loved to iron the finished articles, smoothing the pillowcases, inhaling the perfumed steam as she worked away, calling the others to admire the whiteness. The beds were works of art when changed ready for the sleepers.

Evelyn liked white blouses and washed them by hand. She stiffened them with a starch made from cornflour, and spent ages ironing the collars to perfection.

"All a waste of time," Chrissie would mumble as she watched the blouses being hung up carefully on hangers. Lavender bags were placed on the hangers to perfume the material. Evelyn's brassieres and underclothing were also steeped in a bucket and washed to a pristine whiteness. The other two women would comment on this procedure, but Evelyn ignored their remarks.

"Yer far too particular. Sure that collar won't last a day, and then it has to be done again."

Annie sometimes went with the other two when they were visiting a particular shop. They were friendly with an assistant there called Carmel. She had been in the shop since she had served her time, years before. Carmel was glamorous with silky blonde hair, and a good figure. Her shapely legs were always encased in silk hosiery, her high heels beating on the wooden floor boards. She would bring out boxes from the shelves behind her.

They were fascinated by her white hands, with long fingers ending in scarlet painted nails. These nails tapped on the wooden counter as they removed the garments from the boxes. All colours shimmered through her hands. Big bulky directoire knickers became like wisps as she weaved them through the air. She would hold up interlock vests to the light and make the lace around the neckline look like something fit for a ball. Their eyes would follow the movements as they were mesmerised by her magical hands.

The young man further along the counter at the men's end was also intrigued by her movements, but they could see as she moved upwards to lift down the boxes where his eyes were swivelling. He was one of their boarders, and he always appeared to them to be so quiet and stayed in every night. Chrissie would alert Evelyn and nod in his direction.

Carmel was an actress and should have been on the stage they thought, as she changed her personality to amuse them. She would sometimes act as if she was drunk and stumble and shimmy down the counter aisle, pretending to be looking for something on the shelves. The women would be doubled up laughing at her antics.

The shop owner was a dried up, papery kind of a man. He was grey haired, grey faced and wore grey suits. He had a fixed smile and neat shiny teeth. His colourless hands could not make magic on the counter, and when he came after Carmel she would walk in front of him sedately, but with her eyes so crossed that the ladies along the counter bent over in spasms of laughter. As he walked along he didn't suspect anything, but just thought he had a jolly shop.

Sometimes Carmel opened her handbag and took a swig of alcohol while the women gasped at her cheek.

"He'll smell you, Carmel…" they would say.

"He'll not smell me now," said Carmel, plucking a piece of parsley out of a shopping basket, chewing it with her eyes crossed.

"But it's sticking between your teeth!"

They loved to watch her deftly roll out the curtain material and measure it against the brass ruler on the counter. The piece cut would be carefully folded and wrapped beautifully in shiny brown paper, tied with string off the roller at the side and finished by a sharp crack as she whipped the piece of string off. The money would be put into a container and whizzed along to the office and sent back with the receipt and change.

All the while Carmel would tell them about where she had been the night before, what she wore and how tight she had been.

"I was high as a kite," was her interpretation of a good night out.

Women always told her to be careful: she was their bright spark in their dull lives. When the laughter got overloud the grey one would amble along, but Carmel knew how to get rid of him. She would whip out lacy brassieres and knickers and hold them up.

"Ladies," he would mutter with his tight smile, and move on.

He would try to get them interested in interlock vests for men, and they would say they hadn't any menfolk. He didn't ask outright for them to recommend his wares to all the boarders. The young chap working there didn't wear the clothes.

"She's like a young sister to us," Chrissie said of Carmel as they left the shop. "I wish we had her as a boarder."

"Catch yerself on!" Annie told her. "Can you imagine the nights we'd be up? It's bad enough with the Fridge Man, but think of him and her comin' home together. It's all right behind a counter – and what about the rest of the chaps? That young one can't take his eyes off her!"

At the next emporium they sometimes visited, the owner had a big bosom and a cleavage that she filled with crystal beads.

"She wears all that perfume to hide sweat, I'm sure," Chrissie told them. "Her cheeks are rouged, and she moves about like a ship in full sail."

Here a hat could be bought for church, or a good dress. Once she got the customer stripped in the cubicle, they were at her mercy. An assistant would be called, for the heavy work of carrying and fetching. Amid the heavy perfume and bright lights of the cubicle, the two women would sweat and gaze at their bodies: bodies that they hadn't seen from maybe last year.

'My, have I put on weight on my hips!' Evelyn thought.

Chrissie just thought that everything was going down fast.

They stuck their arms out through the curtains to receive more dresses, and to hand out those they had tried on.

"Come out, Miss Tracey, till I get a look at you," said the shop owner.

Evelyn would appear and Annie, who was seated on a chair at the counter, either nodded or shook her head as she viewed the apparition in front of her. The shop owner tweaked and smoothed the material on the back of the dress.

"You look ravishing, positively ravishing," gushed the shop owner.

Annie's eyes nearly went up under her hat. Annie had always liked hats, especially the round straw one that she plonked squarely on her head, catching the elastic band under her tight grey bun. These were her 'goin' to meetin' hats'. Brooches also were important to her. But Evelyn was the dresser!

"How much is it?" Annie asked, changing the subject.

"Now, I'll have to see. What about the other Miss Tracey?"

Chrissie never came out. She always made up her own mind in the cubicle and tossed the one she had chosen on the counter.

"How much?" she would ask tersely.

When the owner set her sights on Annie, the older woman always got up from the chair and made for the door. On one occasion the owner followed her out, and Annie hid around the corner.

"Your mother's disappeared!" the shop owner cried.

"Just as well, before she heard the price of these outfits!" replied Evelyn.

"How much will you make them?" Evelyn always said when the price was given.

After much tittering and flustering, the owner struck a price. Parcels under their arms, they all made for home.

"Don't let the boarders see the parcels," cautioned Evelyn, "for they'll think we have money to burn and are charging them too much."

The garments were relegated to the back hall, to be brought out at night, when they would dress up and view themselves from all angles in the hall mirror.

"All dressed up and nowhere to go," Annie would tell them.

"Well, there's the church tea." Evelyn always dressed for the church.

# CHAPTER EIGHTEEN

## The Ash Pit Run

The women hated to deal with the ashes. A man came around with a horse and cart to remove all the waste and the ashes from the back yards of the houses. Most of them had ash pits, which were filled and packed down with cinders. The boarding house had such a tiny yard that it wasn't possible to have an ash pit. Chrissie was in charge of this waste, and she filled buckets and tubs and other utensils with the endless panfuls of the grey gritty stuff, that she had to carry from the two open fireplaces. Wet days were better than any windy days, as when she would open the back door the light soft material would *whish* up into her face and hair. The other two never could make out what words she used, as she conveyed her important cargo across the hall, manoeuvring through furniture and shouting to the others to open the back door. Evelyn would turn her back to the offending pan.

"It's all right for you," Chrissie told her. "I get all the dirty work, and those lazy men in there watch me without getting off their backsides to help."

She'd lower the pan to shove the ashes into a bucket gently, and then cover the bucket with paper which was weighed down by a brick. This was an unsatisfactory way of keeping the waste. A part from the unsightly rows of buckets and tubs, the women were always afraid of rats gathering there. When too much had accumulated there would be a heated conference over endless cups of tea, while they gazed out of the back door.

"A body could trip over so many buckets and get a lamater," said Annie, who was always so frightened of falling.

Evelyn told them that she had heard that people from the town were starting to carry their ashes to the old bridge and tipping them into the river.

"That's scandalous!" said Annie, staring at Evelyn. "Who does it?"

"They didn't say, but it's worth thinking about."

Chrissie was so fed up with the rows of buckets that she held the warm cup of tea up to her mouth, screwed up her eyes and thought about the way to get rid of her gritty cargo in the yard.

"What do ye think about it Evelyn? Are ye game to try?" asked Chrissie. "Isn't it a pity we couldn't get some of our boarders to carry a bucket each. Can you imagine the Fridge Man with one in each hand, staggering up the street spillin' all round him? We'll ask the younger ones. Us carrying two buckets each would only get rid of four."

"I'm not havin' any part nor parcel in this," said Annie, setting her cup down. "Ye'll be lifted by the Police."

"'Middle aged ladies up for ash clearance trip'," Chrissie giggled. "We'll be in the papers."

"It's no laughin' matter. What will the minister say?" asked Annie.

"Maybe he has his own ash run with yon wife of his," said Evelyn, as she rocked back in her chair.

The seeds of the way to get rid of their abundance of waste were sown and Evelyn and Chrissie decided to do a trial run.

"We'll dress up in old clothes," Chrissie decided.

"I haven't got any old clothes," Evelyn told her.

"What about the Fridge Man's overalls? They're clean in the hot press."

Chrissie got the garment out, and Evelyn stepped into the navy outfit. Chrissie had chosen the largest buckets and secured the ashes down firmly with newspapers. It seemed to be a calm night. Gripping the handles of the buckets firmly, the two women went through the front door, dancing nervously up and down the street to make sure that it was clear of late night walkers. Annie watched anxiously from the doorway.

"Such a carry on," she kept murmuring to herself.

The two women had a five-minute walk before they would reach the bridge over the river.

"*The buckets are beating against my legs,*" Evelyn whispered to Chrissie.

"*Hold them out from you,*" Chrissie panted back.

"I'm pounded. This is nonsense. What do we do if we meet anybody?" asked Evelyn.

"Just keep walking," said Chrissie.

"There's somebody comin', and by the step of him he's drunk!" said Evelyn.

"It's the Fridge Man. Holy Mackerel, we're done for!" cried Chrissie.

The stumbling figure approached them and stopped.

"Is that you Chrissie? Who's your friend?"

Evelyn walked on.

"Are those my overalls?"

He began to weave after Evelyn and reached out for one of her buckets.

"What's in there?" He grappled among the newspapers and brought out a handful of cinders. Then he peered into her face above the overalls.

"Evelyn is that you? Am I seeing things? The two of you with buckets of ashes! What's up?"

He rocked backwards and forwards viewing the women.

"Walk on, Chrissie!" insisted Evelyn.

Some of the ashes were escaping from the bucket disturbed by the drunken hands. As they moved off the Fridge Man weaved after them.

"Get on back home to yer bed!" cried Evelyn.

He still kept on and began to try to reach for the buckets.

"I'll give you a hand. Where are you going?"

"To the river," Evelyn got out as she trudged on. "Keep your hands off."

She swung round and the bucket in her right hand coped over. The ashes spewed out along with tins and bottles. The Fridge Man walked into the mess and tripped, falling into it. Chrissie put her load down and tried to haul him up, but his feet kept slipping in the ashes.

"I'm scraped and cut," he kept telling them. "This is a nightmare."

They got him to his feet finally and propped him against a wall.

"Stand there till we come back."

He began to grind his teeth.

"That will keep him occupied till we come back. Let the stuff lie."

They hauled their load to the top of the bridge and let the remaining three buckets down.

"Isn't the river lovely at this time of the night?"

"Don't waste time, Chrissie. Help me haul this bucket up to balance it on the wall," said Evelyn.

They got it up and Evelyn slipped off the paper cover.

"There's a bit of wind, so try to throw the stuff over after it blows."

They emptied the contents one and the wind brought gritty ash back onto their faces and hair and eyes, Evelyn kept rubbing her eyes and blinking hard.

"I've got more of it in my eyes."

She tried to wipe them but couldn't find the grit. Two more bucket loads went over with the same backlash.

"We're some sight!" Evelyn's cheeks were covered with streaks of tears and soot.

"Never again, look at the cut of us," said Chrissie.

The buckets clanked and clattered as they swung them around their legs on their way back.

"He's still propped up on that wall," said Chrissie. "He's some sight too, with all that waste he fell into. Would we need to wash him?"

"No way! We'll have enough bother getting ourselves clean," said Evelyn. "I'll have to wash this long hair of mine and how will I get it dried at this time of night?"

"He'll dirty the bedclothes if he gets in that state," said Chrissie.

"Do you fancy bathing him? He'll do tonight," stated Evelyn.

They got the Fridge Man to walk beside them and he kept bumping into the buckets.

"That's right, waken the whole neighbourhood!" said Evelyn. "Who's that at our door talking to Annie? It's that swanky dame from next door. Just keep walking on. Keep the buckets in front of you. Good evening! Nice night."

Annie watched, amazed at the figures coming through the doorway. Evelyn's hair had come down from her top knot. Her face was filthy, the dungarees were dirty. Chrissie's hair was like a birch frizz and her lisle tights were wrinkled around her thick ankles. The Fridge Man just looked a mess. His jacket was white with ash and he stumbled past her.

"All home and accounted for," Annie smiled at the astonished face of the neighbour, whose eyebrows were now up under her posh hat.

"I'll lock up. Good night to you," she edged the door closed and stood against it to watch the group making its way to the kitchen. "Yer lucky ye weren't lifted the lot of ye. Didn't I warn ye?! Look at the hall floor!"

# CHAPTER NINETEEN

## A Dog's Life

"There will be no more dogs here. We have enough two-legged trouble without another dog."

Chrissie had a love for dogs. They all had, but their accommodation wasn't suitable. Chrissie had gone out for the milk to the front door and there stood the leanest greyhound she had ever seen. It was a slate grey colour with such a long pointed nose, ending in a dry snout. It watched her, with wide, wise eyes. A bus driver stopped and told her that some gypsies had camped in a tent by the old school, and they must have moved on, leaving the dog. Its nose was covered in blood. Some boys had attacked it with saucepans left beside the open fire they had used. The body looked so big: how could she get it into the house without the others knowing? Annie always lamented about the lurcher they already had, sleeping in the kitchen in front of the cooker.

"I'll break my leg some day jumping over that thing."

Chrissie had to think quickly about how she could to get shelter for the dog. The family car, the old Morris Minor, 'Emo' they called it, was parked under an old tree. Lifting the keys from the hall table and calling the dog over to the car, Chrissie got the animal inside. It threw its body down on the back seat and skelleyed up at Chrissie.

"Where is it?" Annie called from the door. "Good riddance. We've enough bother."

Chrissie's bothers were only starting. She had to make an excuse to give the dog water and some food. The vet got his breakfast and Chrissie used awkward sign language to explain that she had a patient in the car. He examined its nose and told her it was not a young dog. Its ears were tattooed. It had been a racer. It was also a bitch.

"My luck," said Chrissie. " If it comes on heat I may leave the town." She could just imagine a pack of slabbering dogs roaming around Emo, and Evelyn dressed in her best going out to the scene. "Where will I put her?"

Chrissie wasn't herself all morning, and the front door and the pavement outside got a lot of attention from a polishing cloth and the sweeping brush. The dog was moving about. She ran over to the car and stood petrified, watching bits of something being whirled about the back. The dog was chewing the back of the passenger seat.

"What'll I do?" she muttered, leaning on the brush gazing in at the mess.

"I'll tell you what you'll do!" Evelyn was standing beside her. Even her eyebrows were bristling. "Get that thing out of there and don't let us become a spectacle."

Annie had come to the door and kept shouting over "What's up?"

Slipping her apron over the dog's neck, Chrissie guided it over to the house. There was blood on its mouth where it had cut its old gums chewing.

"Och, the poor animal." Annie had seen the blood. "Bring it in, it's hurt."

She hadn't seen the car. Chrissie hurried quickly past her into the kitchen and the dog lay down in front of the cooker. It was exhausted with its work on the seat, and Annie mistook this for simple tiredness.

"Poor old thing," said Annie. "I'll get it a drink. Look at the cut of its nose with blood. Somebody's hit it."

A dish of food was laid beside it and the wise eyes viewed them as it nosed its way through the plateful.

"It would eat sharpin' stones, that one."

Annie was talking to the dog, and Chrissie knew that if she approved, the animal would become another boarder. She waited for the onslaught from Evelyn, who now stood at the door.

"I'll pay for all the damage," Chrissie muttered as she moved next to Evelyn. "Don't tell Annie."

Evelyn nodded and watched Annie stroke the dog's head.

"What'll we call her?" asked Annie. She started going over all the names she could remember. The dog raised its head when she called 'Sheelagh'. "That's it! She's a Sheelagh. You'll have to take it out with Brandy. Does it need a muzzle?"

Evelyn was wetting the tea. "*Does it need a muzzle?*" she repeated. Chrissie shook her head at her.

"I'll find out. If only it would lie under the table."

Annie got some old cardigans and made a bed for it. The dog moved onto the soft pile of clothes and arranged itself, with its nose on the big paws.

"It said in the Bible about a greyhound," Annie told them. "An' it's got the head of a snake and tail of a mouse."

Right enough its whip like tail was a disappointing end to the deep waisted body.

The lurcher Brandy walked in and went over to sniff Sheelagh. The greyhound didn't move; she just kept watching. This was the big test. Chrissie washed dishes and noted that Brandy walked stiffly over to the cooker, plonking herself down facing the newcomer.

"The jobs a good 'un," Chrissie said to herself.

Sheelagh had settled in well.

"What's that dog doin' up those stairs?"

They could hear a bumping noise from the second floor, and

Chrissie mounted the steps with fear in her eyes. Sheelagh was in the Fridge Man's bedroom. Pieces of a book were lying about, and the dog had a bit sticking out of her mouth.

"What have you been at!" The hard back of the book lay at the door. "Holy Mackerel! It's his Robbie Burns poetry book!"

This was his Bible. He quoted from it, sang from it and lived by it.

"What'll I do?" Chrissie gathered up the pieces and tried to smooth them out. The dog lay watching her. "Why did you do it? Why did you slip upstairs?"

Sheelagh passed her and went awkwardly down the stairs, big grey feet stopping at each step. Chrissie followed, her face a picture of misery.

"Why am I afflicted like this?" she moaned. "I'm good to that dog. I got it in here. The Fridge Man'll go stark ravin' mad."

No money could replace that book. It was his grandfather's. She held the bit out in front of her and slipped into the kitchen.

"Wait till I tell you what's happened."

Chrissie sat down heavily at the kitchen table and told the other two about the catastrophe.

"I'll explain to him what happened," said Evelyn, standing at the cooker. "It's not the end of the world. Chrissie, contain yourself. Your blood pressure is high enough without this. It's only a book. Listen, dog," she held out her wooden spoon to the big animal, "you've committed a crime this day, and it'll take some explaining to this man. If only you could tell me where you found the book, so we can make up some story to get out of this pickle."

Evelyn thought for a moment.

"Chrissie: who made the beds this morning?"

"I did."

"Did you notice where the book was sittin'?"

"He always kept it in the bedside locker."

"Could it have been tipped into the waste paper basket?" Chrissie's eyes lit up.

"I'll be the one who'll take the blame. But look, we'll just never say anything. Never let on. If he's as drunk as usual he'll not know what he's done with it."

"We hope," said Annie. "If it comes to the crunch I'd rather have the dog than him anyway."

# CHAPTER TWENTY

## 'It or Me'

Sheelagh the greyhound watched with wise eyes. The dog didn't move. Annie glanced at the ceiling.

"Maybe he'll quit that singin' he does if he forgets the words, and no book to refer to. Look at the handlin' that night we had to heave him up the stairs."

Evelyn moved away from the cooker.

"That pan's too hot, the smeech rising up from it will ruin my hair, and my eyes are smarting. Bring that ham out of the oven. It's ready now."

"Look behind ye, there's an apparition appearin' through the smeech," Annie muttered as she busied herself at the table.

The Fridge Man stood in the doorway. His cheeks were an unhealthy pinky red; the bloodshot eyes were nearly bolting out of his head. He kept clearing his throat and swallowing big gulps of air. Torn pages were held out in front of the barrel chest. He made no reference to the book.

"Either that dog goes, or I do."

He pulled himself up to face the three women.

Evelyn noted that he had scraped his thinning grey hair back with a wide toothed comb to face them. The dog didn't move, just watched the scene. Annie sat down. This was the first time they had faced a situation like this.

Evelyn moved to stand in front of William, leaving the pan to Chrissie who stood leaning on the cooker minding the food.

Chrissie was torn between stirring the gravy in the pan and gleekin' at the irate figure in the doorway. Nobody spoke. Annie gathered a few crumbs off the table with her hand and dropped them to the dog. Chrissie turned back to the cooker and skelleyed sideways at Annie. Evelyn stood facing the boarder. The women hadn't consulted one another about how to handle the situation when it would arise, but each of them had arrived at the same decision. Evelyn's voice when it came out had the polite accent that she used when answering the phone.

"I'm sorry about Robbie Burns, but Sheelagh stays."

The man's face nearly crumpled. He'd left himself no way back in his statement. These people had been good to him. He thought of the warm bed with the hot water bottle waiting for him every night, the good food and the way they helped him when he came in drunk. The women felt sorry for him, but the situation was there. They had enough to contend with, without worrying about keeping him sweet.

"I'll leave at the end of the week." He hung on, leaning his hand on the table, gazing at each face in turn hoping that they would take pity on him, and plead with him to stay. The blank faces told him that their decision had been made. He turned his back and walked up the hall, his steps getting slower. As he passed the 'fridge phone' it rang, and he answered it.

"That'll be another bit of bother out of the way," Chrissie said to Evelyn in a loud voice so he could hear. "And to think he wanted rid of our Sheelagh."

Evelyn carried the food tray down the hall towards the dining room. She walked slowly past him so he could get a good whiff of the roast ham, apple stuffing, home made gravy and roast potatoes. His favourite dinner would be set down for him tonight. Where would he be eating next week? She paused to ask him to open the door so he could get a close up of the food.

"*Make sure that phone of yours is out of here by Friday,*" she whispered.

The open fire beside the dining room table glowed with the coal and blocks banked up to welcome the boarders. All these home comforts would be sorely missed.

The work began in the kitchen again. Annie got up to help Chrissie at the cooker.

"That's put me out of my way of goin'." She slapped the kettle down hard and her face was hot. "We have little need of this carry on."

"Don't fuss yourself, Mother. We didn't do anything wrong," said Evelyn. "I've told him to take the phone out by Friday."

Annie hadn't thought of that. Such a relief not to suffer the shrill screech of that instrument going through her head.

They heard him thumping up the stairs and banging about his room. The women sat down at the table. Annie took off her glasses and wiped her eyes. Evelyn smoothed her hair back and Chrissie sucked a sugar lump.

"That was a carry on. The dog was wrong, but he's not going to take over: demanding that Sheelagh should go!" Chrissie slipped a sugar lump into the dog's mouth under the table. "There won't be many to take him in."

"Chrissie, you're getting fat," Evelyn said, trying to lighten the situation.

"You've pillions of fat under yer arms," said Annie, peering through her glasses at Chrissie.

"I'm all right," said Chrissie, who never wanted her body looked at. "We can't all be like Evelyn the model here."

# CHAPTER TWENTY-ONE

## 'Doctor Dear'

Every day Chrissie and Evelyn took the dogs for exercise, around the side of the house and down a long lane where they could run freely. They were able to discuss things without Annie interfering. They all loved one another, but were living so close together and the work was so heavy, that tempers flared up. Yet they were a team of three against the boarders. They needed the money, but hated the way their house was taken over.

On one occasion a neighbour and her dog met them on the laneway, and their lurcher took a dislike to the other dog. They flew at one another and Chrissie said afterwards that she could see the hair flying off the poodle type dog. She rushed in to separate them and got bitten on the hand. The neighbour, who was fussily dressed (complete with hat), fell back into the hedge. The hat came off and Chrissie could see 'she was scarce of hair', as she put it. The woman got herself sorted and strutted up the lane, promising that they would hear more about it, and then all would be let loose.

'What did she mean?' Chrissie wondered, visualising policemen, solicitors and the court house.

Chrissie had to go to the doctor with the bite. He cleaned the wound and gave her an injection. As he escorted her to the door, the doctor enquired about the type of boarder she kept.

"Were they a nice class?" he asked.

Chrissie thought of the Fridge Man and nearly burst out

laughing, thinking of them hauling him upstairs when he was drunk.

"What do you mean?" she answered, straightening her back to give herself confidence.

"I have a young locum, and would need accommodation for him."

"Send him over and we'll have a look at him," was her reply as she made for the door. "*What class of boarder do we keep?* indeed!" she kept repeating to the others. "It's money we want, to pay our way. Class doesn't come into it."

A young man arrived one afternoon and Evelyn kept him at the door.

"It's the classy doctor," she informed the others in the kitchen.

"Keep him hanging on for a while. Don't rush out."

"He's wild young looking – I wouldn't have much faith in him. He wanted to know if we had a garage for his car!"

"We haven't even got a shed," they laughed.

Evelyn told him he could have a room and he shook her hand. She came in holding her hand out to tell the others.

"I thought he was going to bow. The Fridge Man will soon knock the manners out of him."

"Does he want a phone?" Annie quavered.

Evelyn said he never mentioned a phone. 'No more phones here,' they all agreed. He settled in and although he could not attend meals on time, they felt he was no different from the others.

He lost his calm demeanour one lunchtime as he chomped his way through a salad.

There was a sound of metal being crushed at the front of the house. He rushed to the door and was in time to see his car being carried along the road by a bus. The side was caved in. The young doctor just stood against the wall and gradually slid down, to sit on his hunkers gazing at the wreck.

"It was nearly new," he kept saying.

"Never mind," said Evelyn as he patted his shoulder, and tried to get him to his feet. As she told the rest afterwards, she thought he was going to cry on her shoulder. "It's only a car. Nobody's hurt."

They led him back into the dining room.

"I don't suppose you want the sponge pudding now," said Annie.

"Annie! The chap's shocked: bring him sweet tea."

"Do ye want to go after your car?" asked Chrissie.

There was a knock at the door. A policeman asked about the owner of the car. Chrissie took him in to the young man now sipping tea. Amid all the questions and answers the women cleared the dinner table, listening to the snippets of conversations.

The Transport people and the Police filled the dining room for quite a while. It was a diversion the women could have done without. The young doctor didn't need it either. He kept saying the car was 'nearly new'.

The women were awakened that night by a loud banging on the front door. After clustering at the top of the stairs, Evelyn broke away and held her hands to her ears as she walked to the door. Their friend the 'dog woman' almost fell in, and stumbled to the newel post at the bottom of the stairs. She had her head against it ('No hat,' they noticed) and gasped out that her dog had just died, and her mother was going to die. She was more upset about the dog. Her son was living with her, but he didn't count. He always strutted along, head in the air and didn't speak to anybody. He had a sense of humour though. They had seen the pieces of paper stuffed into empty milk bottles carrying the milk order. The other side of the papers depicted stick people in all sorts of activities. One stick person was sitting on a toilet with trousers wrinkled around his feet. Annie had sympathised with this one.

The boarders were gathered at the top of the stairs, peering at the scene down below. Evelyn nearly clapped her hands to get them to disperse. Chrissie helped the woman into the kitchen, where she collapsed into a chair. Her dressing gown was of good quality they noticed, and her slippers had heels – no soft flat ones with pom poms like Annie's. It was a pity about her thin hair, Evelyn thought. Her cries lessened as Annie patted her back. Tea was made.

"The dog was old," Annie sympathised.

"So is my mother; and I'm sixty-five! What will I do with myself?"

Annie, who was over eighty, nearly told her that they could do with help with the boarders. She herself never had a minute. The visitor began to rise from the chair. Her old withdrawn, haughty look was coming back. Drawing her dressing gown around her she moved to the door, as if it was just an ordinary social visit. Evelyn walked behind her up the hall and opened the door.

"You'll be all right now?"

"Of course. How stupid of me to make such a fuss. Sorry to disturb you."

At each word she walked on until she reached her own door. With a regal wave of her hand she disappeared.

"What a carry on," said Annie, swirling the dregs of her tea around the bottom of the cup to soak up the last of the sugar. "She walked out as if she had a pole stuck up her back. Only it's a pity of her right enough. She only has her pride."

The kitchen grew quiet, as they sat thinking about the woman, and also the young doctor having the mishap with his car.

Evelyn's car was an extended part of their house. Annie practically worshipped it, as well as the cooker. She watched it from the front window, always taking note of other cars being parked near it. The women would go out with buckets of water and sponges to keep it clean. They would carry the old Hoover to it, laying a trap for unsuspecting walkers, with the electric lead lying across the pavement. As Evelyn whipped the lead around to get to the odd corners in the car, Chrissie would shout to her that she wasn't insured for being in charge of a Hoover on the road. Annie would worry about the tyres ('Were they worn?' 'Was the water topped up in the radiator?'). Anti-freeze was a big worry for her. She would watch the weather and rush out late at night with big newspapers to place around the windscreen. A kettle was used on frosty mornings to defrost the keyhole, and to trickle over the windows. When she was being driven anywhere, a noise in the car would set her off, and the mechanic would be round to investigate. She would discuss the 'rattle', as she called it. It would either be a sharp or dull noise and she trusted him like a doctor to cure the patient.

Evelyn didn't know anything about the Highway Code – her licence had been given to her on application. When she went into shops for big bags of flour and groceries, the car was left in the middle of the street. The local Police always said she didn't park the car, she abandoned it. The car would stop dead, out of petrol: it was the last thing they would think about. The mechanic, when called would remind her once again to 'fill her up'. They hated to part with money, yet they needed the car.

If Evelyn or Chrissie met a boarder when they were out, they didn't speak to them. It was part of their odd thinking. These men had to live in the house with them, but were not part of their lives outside.

Annie seldom went in the car except sometimes to church, and she expected it to go on forever. One morning she didn't get up.

"I feel drowsy," she kept telling them.

"Not like her," Chrissie told Evelyn as they viewed her. The blankets were pulled up to just below her small red nose.

"Leave me be. I'll be up later on."

"If the doctor chap is still in, we'll get him to look at her. If not, maybe the vet would give her the once over."

Evelyn and Chrissie were worried. Like the car and the cooker, they expected Annie to go on forever. The doctor was just going out of the door when Evelyn nabbed him.

"Would you look at my Mother, please? She's not feeling well."

The young chap changed into Doctor's style as he mounted the stairs.

"How long has she been sick?"

"Never had treatment in her life," replied Evelyn.

"What medication is she on?"

Evelyn thought of the big pile of Regulette boxes and decided not to mention them.

"Never takes medicine."

Annie could not be coaxed from under the bedclothes. The only symptoms she mentioned were a sore throat. The doctor wrote out a prescription for an antibiotic, which Annie told them later to put in the bin. Some days later she announced she felt a bit better, and came shakily downstairs.

"It's the bowel tablets she wants." The two women had kept them off her when she was off her feet.

"I've sent for the older doctor. The *real* one." Annie would rather have him.

The mature man gave Annie a thorough examination, and announced that he thought she had had a heart attack.

"A *what*?" Annie went from feeling fear to pride. "And I never knew."

"Just be good to her," he told the two shocked daughters, "and don't let her climb those stairs."

Now Annie had something to talk about as well as her bowels.

The heart was a respectable subject, and she began to wonder who would carry her upstairs. Two boarders, the stronger ones, were selected at tea time to carry her up to the bedroom.

"Now I know how the Fridge Man felt. Put me down. I've still the power of my legs."

Visitors came to see her. The chaps would put heads around the bedroom door, to ask her how she felt. 'They're not so bad,' she thought, as she gave them instructions to bring up a cup of tea, tell Evelyn or Chrissie she wanted them and many other things she wanted them to do. They were glad when the doctor said she could come down among them all again.

"The kitchen looks that bright," she announced, as they set her in the corner by the cooker, "and the boarders look that big."

"You've only been in bed ten days, Mother."

Evelyn and Chrissie were so glad to see their mother in the kitchen again. They watched her sweel her hair up lightly into the usual knot at the back.

"We were thinking, what with you upstairs sick and us short-handed, we would need central heating. It would do away with the open fire, the carting up of coal and sticks and anthracite from the cellar."

'Would they have to touch the cooker?' Annie was excited at the thought of men working at the innards of her old friend. Evelyn shook her head at Chrissie.

"Don't discuss it now."

The workmen arrived and took over the house. They were a rough looking lot, the women decided as they watched them troop into the hallway. Work bags were flung on the floor, tools clanking inside. The men moved quickly around the rooms, eyes roving over the space, bending down exposing big fat buttocks under pale washed jeans.

"Did you ever see the like of them?" Chrissie watched, amazed at the quick movements of these workmen.

They spent a long time in the cellar, banging about shifting things around. They called each woman 'Mrs' as they asked questions. Evelyn supervised the moving of furniture, and inwardly cringed as she heard pieces of carpet being ripped off and floor boards prised up. The *noise* had begun.

"Do they use a hammer in every hand?" Annie moaned as the pounding began.

Raw metal sounds also filled the ears as machines cut pipes. Smells from blow lamps and soldering equipment clogged their noses, and the dust that settled everywhere.

"If we had somewhere to go…" Chrissie always muttered standing at the open door. They never closed it, these men. She complained it was open to the wind and the whole country could look in. The air outside was so fresh and sweet. Evelyn was worried about what people would say about the state of the place. Anyone passing could see right in. The hall was full of 'rads' as the men called the radiators. A younger member of the team had a wireless that blared loudly above the rest of the noises: Evelyn flinched as she knew that anyone passing got full blast of the pop songs.

"I'm not feeding this lot, Chrissie. So don't even mention feeding times to them."

Evelyn couldn't believe her eyes when she saw them all clustered in the kitchen around Annie, who was feeding them hot pancakes off the griddle.

"What's the good in talking?" Chrissie mused as they watched.

The house wasn't theirs anymore. Annie couldn't perch on the lavatory for any length of time, as there would be a rattle on the door handle when one of the men wanted to work on the pipes. Her lovely linen and towels were tossed about the hot press as big hands tumbled them, getting at the copper tank.

Finally all was in place and the oil ordered. The heat was wonderful. Now there were so many places to dry things. Another worry for Annie was 'When will the oil dry up, when will we know?' Also there were rattling noises over the old house, as the heating warmed walls and flooring.

"Those chaps were company during the day," Annie announced when they finally left. "They put a radiator right beside the lavatory seat for me!"

# CHAPTER TWENTY-TWO

## Evelyn's Beau

Annie was getting older: her joints were stiff, particularly her knees. She would lift her skirt to view them, and ask the others to look at them to see if one was more swollen than the other.

"Wrap a cabbage leaf around them. It helped the last time. There's work in you yet!" Chrissie in particular hadn't much sympathy.

Knobbly knees were encased in thick stockings, which were sweeled into a loop and secured with a button. When a button dropped – as it frequently did – Annie went around the floor with a sweeping brush, pushing the other two women out of the way, moaning about her loss. She liked the buttons; they were mother-of-pearl ones she had cut off an old coat, and she always said they just did the job. Evelyn would come into the kitchen, with a visitor or boarder, to find Annie with her lisle stockings wrinkled around her feet, bent double in her search.

"Mother!" she would say, through tight lips. "Here's somebody to see you," and Annie would prop the brush against the dresser and get her legs under the table.

"She'd affront you scrambling about there for a button," Evelyn would remark. "It's wonderful how she can bend when she wants to."

Annie was always frightened of not being able to walk, so she tried to keep on the move. When she had a new ache or pain she'd inform the others that something had to come to take her away.

"Aren't we here to look after you?" her daughters would reply.

Evelyn and Chrissie were not ever going to leave her – Annie knew that. They loved her. She was the reason Evelyn had not got married. An engineer had arrived from England to work at a pig factory in the city, and he and Evelyn had started to talk when he came in for his meals. Chrissie and Annie had watched amazed, as Evelyn had smiled at this man, Charles. She had never had any lengthy conversations before with any boarder, and was definitely not on 'smiling terms' with them.

"He's a cut above the rest; he knows his place," Evelyn would say, as the engineer's plate was heaped with extra bacon and mushrooms for breakfast. She took his laundry to the cleaners for him.

"Doesn't he smell nice and clean?"

The other two women would repeat these words and smirk behind Evelyn's back.

One evening Evelyn got ready to go out. This was *so* unusual.

"The shops are shut," Annie told her.

"I know, but I'm going out for a run with Charles. He has something to do at the plant, and it would do me good to get out."

She wore her high heels, good blouse and skirt. Evelyn's hair never came down or frizzed when she worked. Her mother often commented on her complexion. "Clear and flushed like a peach,' Annie would say when she wanted to praise her. "Of course it wasn't for the want of creams that she used." Evelyn had neat ankles and looked after her hands and nails.

"This is serious," Chrissie said as they watched her get into Charles' car. They sat in the kitchen and watched the clock.

"She's fifty-nine," Annie said, "and can come and go."

But numerous cups of tea were swallowed during the two hours Evelyn was away. Chrissie served supper to the boarders, slapping the tray down on the table, nearly knocking the home baked pastries off the plates. What would they do, if Evelyn went to England? How would she look after their Mother? Maybe he was married and had a family? What had possessed Evelyn? Was he older than her?

Annie sat in the kitchen counting the Regulettes pills. Would he be good to her? She would be for the old folk's home for sure now. At eighty years of age she was going down hill.

"We'll not mention anything to her," Chrissie said.

"I'm not going to bed till she comes in," Annie said firmly. "Do ye think any of the neighbours saw her getting into the car? What possessed her anyway? We got that wee TV and she has the wireless."

Chrissie had no space in her life for romance. She had never been popular with the opposite sex, and she could feel her years going on, endlessly looking after these boarders who would have lives when they moved on. She used to spend time in the library, choosing novels filled with love, lust and passion. As the librarian stamped the books, Chrissie always thought of how another uneventful week of her life had passed. She read the books late at night and tried not to let Annie or Evelyn see the lurid covers.

Chrissie liked to look clean and neat, but she hadn't any style. Her hair was thin and she kept it tightly permed and brightly coloured. She called the treatment she gave it a 'rinch'. Her gait was hampered by the fact that she was knock-kneed. Sometimes she caught sight of herself in the dressing mirror, and cowered under the bedclothes. She regretted that her legs were not straight; when she was younger she had tried to make them straight by skipping up and down steps. 'I'm not knock-kneed,' she'd tell herself, but photographs always showed the fault.

Every time the front door opened the two women jumped. At midnight Annie was yawning and tired.

"I've a good mind to lock the door," said Chrissie." She never took a key. Maybe they've had an accident. If we could use that phone I'd phone the hospital."

"Would he take advantage of her?" Annie cried.

"Our Evelyn?" Chrissie laughed. "Catch yourself on, Mother. She'd clobber him."

"But he's English, far too crafty for her."

"Well she'll not have a wean, anyway," Chrissie giggled at that, and hid in the scullery, laughing at the idea of Evelyn getting pregnant and trying to hide her situation from the boarders. Wouldn't the folk wonder which boarder it was? She held onto the sink doubled up with mirth. The Fridge Man had already asked her to marry him the night she hauled him to bed.

Evelyn arrived in the kitchen, bringing the cool night air on her clothes.

"What kept ye?" Annie could hardly contain herself. "Have ye taken leave of yer senses?"

"I enjoyed the run," Evelyn said, pouring herself a cup of tea. "He's an interesting man and he would like to take me out again, but I'm not going. It doesn't do to fraternise with the boarders, though he's not a regular. What were you laughing at, Chrissie, when I came in?"

"Just somethin' we were talking about."

Annie went to bed, happy that she still had a home. Evelyn had passed up her chance for romance.

Chrissie slept with Annie. The arrangement had been made to save a room for a boarder, and then they decided to still share a bed. Chrissie slept on the wall side, allowing Annie to get up easily during the night. They had to retire together. Annie insisted on this. The bedside table held Annie's Chlorodyne sweets, and Chrissie kept her favourite brandy balls under her pillow. Annie rattled the strong sweets around her false teeth as she read a chapter of the Bible, her glasses on the end of her wee red nose. Chrissie always remarked on the strength of these sweets, and said the smell of them was enough to knock her out, let alone the powerful burning taste Annie must suffer.

"Never you mind, I'll thole them, and watch you don't choke on your brandy balls."

Evelyn slipped quietly into the bedroom. The two heads propped up on the feather pillows watched her move over to her part of the bedroom. She had a single bed occupying the recess beside the fireplace. She was always self conscious when she started to undress in front of the others. Tonight she had on her special underwear, so she opened the wardrobe door and stripped behind it for privacy.

"I wonder what she has that's different from the rest of us?" Annie would mutter between sucks at her Chlorodynes.

Evelyn let her hair down from the bun when she pulled on her cambric nightdress. She felt free in her nightdress, became a lovely woman. Her silverbacked hair brush stroked the long wavy mass as she leaned forward to let the blood rush to her head – good for the scalp she thought. She swung the nightdress around, enjoying the faint perfume of Yardley's April Violets that came from her body. The white sheets on the bed welcomed her. She couldn't be bothered with a man. Tonight was fun but she needed this freedom. She thought so much of herself. The chocolates on the bedside cabinet were dark Belgian, luxurious pieces that were rationed by her, just two every night. She would feel them, turning them over with her long fingers, sniffing at the rich spicy smell of them. Marzipan and ginger centres were her favourites. Hand and face cream were stroked on before she said her prayers.

What to pray for? She wanted to live a long healthy life, and also prayed for this for her mother and sister. She didn't pray for the boarders except that she needed a plentiful supply coming through the door. A prayer was said every night for her to get the strength to stand them – especially the Fridge Man.

Chrissie always felt the world was secure when she heard Annie mutter through the mouthful of beige coloured Chlorodynes.

"What'll I make for the 'morra's dinner?"

The thought of loneliness always haunted her, and she loved the old woman by her side.

"Did you let the dog out?" Annie would ask her before they went to sleep.

# CHAPTER TWENTY-THREE

## Legs under the Table

"There's something going on in that room."

Evelyn shoved the bags of groceries onto the kitchen table and rushed down the hallway. She had heard thumping, moans and grunts, coming from the sitting room. Their mother had been left there while the Evelyn and Chrissie had gone to shop. This happened once a week, and the old lady had always been secure and happy for the short time on her own.

Evelyn wrenched open the door, but she could not see her mother as usual, sitting in the big chair by the fireside. There was a tangle of legs under the circular dining table, mixed up with the legs of the chairs. Annie's big felt slippers were off, her white knees exposed above the pop socks the sisters had got her to wear. A pair of grey flannel covered legs were feebly moving about near her. A cloth cap lay on her slippers. A walking stick lay on top of her, and another sturdy stick was in held a man's hand. Both were trying to get up, but were so tangled together that this was proving impossible. Evelyn and Chrissie both got down on their hands and knees and crawled under the table, trying to separate the bodies.

"This is a handling," Annie whimpered.

The wire framed glasses on her forehead looked like two more eyes, and her cheeks were pink with exertion. They could see now that the grey flannel legs belonged to Sam, an old man who came for his meals.

"Don't move, Mother! Stop thrashing about, Sam!"

The two younger women were now sweating and wrestling with the chair legs.

"If we haven't the strength to pull them out lengthwise, we'll push them!" Evelyn shouted. "We need help."

They sat back on their hunkers and surveyed the struggling pair.

"We could break a leg here, or an arm," Chrissie warned.

"Maybe they are broke already."

Evelyn thought of the two policemen in the hut in the street just above the house, guarding the town against the Troubles.

"We give them enough cups of tea – they owe us a favour. Run up for them."

Whimpers and moans came from under the table. The two heads were close together, and Evelyn thought to herself how different faces looked without glasses and when lying flat on the ground. Annie was eighty-seven and Sam not far behind.

"Maybe the Police help would not be a good idea. Could we be taken up for neglect? How would we explain the pair under the table? There wasn't any sense to be got out of them in their present shocked state."

Evelyn sat back to think about the situation.

A young policeman arrived and viewed the scene. He spoke to the two under the table.

"Hello there. We'll soon have you on your feet. How's Sam? You'll be glad to get a wee half 'un at the hotel."

"We need more help to lift Sam," he gave orders quietly. The other policeman came and together they manoeuvred the elderly pair legs-first, and then they slid the bodies along the carpet. Both were pulled out and the policemen's hats tumbled off as they bent under the table.

"Ease them up gently to the sitting position. They'll be dizzy."

They held the two old folk up. When they could talk, Evelyn asked them what they were doing under the table.

"I opened the door on my way out," Sam whispered, "to ask your Mother how her diabetes was, and she couldn't hear me. She got up to meet me – I went over to hear her and we got our sticks entwined, staggered about and fell, and then we waltered about trying to get up."

Evelyn looked at the grey trousers.

"He's wet himself," she noted. "Oh, our lovely lemon carpet. Don't let Sam sit down on that good chair, his backside's soakin'."

"Well what will I do with him?" Chrissie was all through-other. She kept wiping away at her forehead.

"Get a chair from the kitchen," Evelyn shouted, "and close the door. I don't want the boarders to see this mess."

Sam kept asking for his stick. It was one James McLaughlin had cut from a hawthorn hedge for him. This was his cherished possession.

"I'm not a bit worried about your stick," said Chrissie. "I am more worried about my sodden carpet." She was now down on her hands and knees, trying to assess the damage. "I wonder will this create a wild smell?"

Evelyn had arrived with a wooden kitchen chair, and shoved Sam onto it.

"Sam, you can't go home with that big wet patch on those light grey trousers. The left leg is completely soaked."

"What about a pair of those navy dungarees belonging to the

Fridge Man to change him into?" Chrissie said, as she sat viewing the sorry sight on the chair.

"I'm not wearing anything belonging to that man," Sam spoke up.

"And I'm sure he wouldn't be too pleased at that bottom of yours going into his working clothes. But this time you'll wear them."

One of the policemen said he would help to strip the culprit. The women turned their backs while he got the trousers off a very irate Sam. Chrissie dumped them into a plastic bag she had brought from the kitchen. The young policeman had bother with Sam's shoes, as the dungarees were tighter than the trousers. The shoes had to be unlaced under directions from Sam. The socks underneath were just a collection of holes.

"An' he looks so decent on the top," remarked Evelyn.

Sam announced he wasn't going to walk home in this apparel. The policeman solved the problem by ordering a Police car to stop and give him a lift. The women were glad to see the odd wee figure disappearing through the door, and turned their attentions to Annie.

"Did you wet yourself, Mother, as well?"

"My bowel mightn't be of the best," Annie shrugged her shoulders in disdain, "but my waterworks are sound. I would like a cup of tea. But wash your hands first."

"I'll make the tea," Evelyn said, "and Chrissie can sponge up the water from the carpet."

"Why do I get all the dirty work?" Chrissie was already down on her hands and knees, trying to soak it up with an old sheet.

"Don't be putting down any of that highly perfumed

disinfectant," Annie muttered as she gazed into the fire. "Do you know? I feel sleepy after all that excitement!"

# CHAPTER TWENTY-FOUR

## Visitors

Visitors were entertained in the good room. To keep the open fire stoked up, the coal scuttle was kept full, and a basket of blocks was piled high near the hearth. Great attention was paid to the tea trolley. Matching starched tray- and trolley cloths were used. Fine china cups and saucers, sparkling teaspoons and a big china teapot were set out.

The guests usually stayed too long, and the busy women had to edge towards the door one by one to disappear into the kitchen to carry on with some necessary chore like starting tea for the sixteen boarders. Finally, one of them – usually Evelyn – would be left making stilted conversation while loud noises, doors slamming, saucepans rattling would come from the kitchen. These were hints to show the visitors to the door.

"Have they nothin' better to do with themselves?!" Annie would rage. "An hour's too long for all that palaver of talk. We should ask them when they come in: 'Is it news you're lookin' for, or a long talk?'"

"There'll be no more of that carry on," Chrissie decided. "The next ones will be shown into the kitchen, set down at the table and take whatever's given. We can work away."

Parents or relations of the boarders liked to visit, to see how their loved one was coping. They usually brought clean shirts and underwear, and boxes of biscuits and home-baked buns.

"More crumbs in the beds and rooms," the women would complain.

"Do they think we don't feed them?" asked Annie, affronted. She would sit chopping vegetables or baking in front of them. Sometimes she would get peeved at the endless questions about how she mixed the ingredients.

"I just put in a gropin' of flour or Indian meal or whatever I'm using," she would reply. Her hands moved deftly and swiftly, and the time was not wasted as the conversation went on.

"Does he sleep at night?" an anxious mother would ask about her young bank clerk son on his first nights away from home.

The women would look at on another. No need to tell the mother that he went out every night at 8pm and they never heard him come in.

"Does he eat well?" was another query. The answer could have been 'he eats well unless he's been drinking the night before'. The boarders were taken aback to see their parents in the kitchen and would flush bright pink at their mothers' adoring glances.

"It takes all sorts," Evelyn always remarked as the folk left. "How did that wee chubby couple produce that big hulkin' chap?"

"Maybe he's not the father!" Annie would cackle.

"Whatever," was Evelyn's reply.

The coal man was a regular visitor. He would breeze in covered in coal dust, having parked his small lorry outside. Evelyn always got him to sit down for tea and fresh baked scones.

"My, them's quare scones."

His black powder-coated fingers flashed the knife as he applied lashings of butter and home made jam.

"He's hungered, that man," Annie always remarked.

She gave him a paper bag with scones to take home. Then the old grating would be lifted and the bags of coal dropped down into the cellar.

"Rush down Chrissie and count the bags, to be sure."

Chrissie would amble down the old stairs and hide behind a wall to count the bags. They had been overcharged by a bag one time and had never forgotten it. They still liked him, but kept themselves right.

The bread man brought plain loaves and anything else they wanted. He hopped into the van with a long pole and hauled out loaves, baps and Paris buns. These were carried in quickly. He always seemed to be in such a hurry. While the coal man was powdered in black dust, this man's coat had white flour on his front. Sometimes his eyelashes and brows were white. He was always peering into his stock on the shelves. His powdery cap was placed carefully on the table, as he sat down to get his ration of home baked bread.

He also brought all the news of the town. Births, deaths, marriages and property sales were the topics most treasured. He also knew the gossip, and the women would pick him about the antics of their boarders, how they acted in the town. Were they courtin'?

On one occasion they nearly kept him all afternoon, to hear about one young person who had dressed up as a woman for a dare, and another who had run across the park stark naked.

"I don't believe it," Annie kept repeating.

"Sure as I'm sitting here – I saw him myself!"

"There's no good in talkin'. His father and mother were sittin' in that chair before you". Annie shoved more bread and butter towards the bread man. "Give him another cup of tea, Evelyn."

The milk man swung his bottles down the hallway, clattering his way in. His horse stopped outside the door and Annie always gave it titbits, patting its head and talking to it. She always got back into the kitchen to hear what his news, was as he supped his tea. They all had different kinds of gossip. The milk man had been up so early he could observe courting couples and accidents.

The weather was always a great topic. He would announce that the motorcars had on chains again for the frosty roads, and warned the women to wear rough socks over their shoes when they went out, as the pavements were like bottles. These men were always welcome. The boarders just gave polite conversation when they came to the kitchen. They didn't seem to be part of the town.

One church member who visited once a month was a woman they did not want to see coming through the door. She was so dry looking – her hair was wispy and dry, and her skin was wrinkled and scaly looking.

"She scrubs at herself too much," Annie said. "That wee nose is so red. It's raw looking. And the eyelashes and brows are white. There isn't even colour in her eyes."

The church lady sat upright on the kitchen chair, viewing all around her. The dry eyes would swivel from the saucepans bubbling on the cooker to the piles of scones resting on the table. She accompanied her spoken words with a loud *sniff* – sometimes two or three. Evelyn hated this habit.

"She has airs and graces that one."

"I do my wash on a Monday, hail, rain or shine," this woman would tell them. "I iron on a Tuesday and bake on a Wednesday."

The three women would collapse laughing when she left, always wondering when she had had time to beget her long thin sons.

A kitten Chrissie which was keeping for a holidaying friend, had been in the kitchen. "Lo and behold," as Annie put it, "it did a wet beside the cooker." The woman looked down in disdain at the tiny puddle.

"Put it in a barrel and drown it!" she said, with a conglomeration of sniffs.

They could hardly wait to show her the door.

"*Dried up old stick!*" Chrissie announced to the kitten, as she held it on her knee and petted it.

Friends from the old days on holidays always called to visit the three women. They sat at the kitchen table and eyes were lit up, faces excited as the conversation began 'do ye mind the time…'

Old times were relived in the kitchen. The light seemed brighter – the kitchen warmer. Old characters were brought to life and the faces around the table were smiling, eyes sparkling as escapades of old were retold, and one storyteller would spark off memories in the others. Evelyn would see their visitors to the door with much hand clasping, shoulder patting and promises to meet again soon. Annie would sit back and hold her glasses up to the light, squinting and wiping to get the tears off them.

"That makes me think long," she told the others. "Those were the days! Folk think they're livin' now. Hard old times, but what fun we had."

She levelled her gaze at the boarder who had waited until the commotion had ceased, who came to ask for two hot water bottles at night instead of one.

"His mother has put him up to that," Annie would insist. "Imagine marryin' a man like that. That chap will never get married. Who'd put up with him? He keeps TCP in his pocket to gargle and put up his nose if anybody sneezes or coughs near him. How could he rear weans?"

Annie's reply to the boarder was to the point:

"If ye buy another bottle I'll fill it for ye," she said, "but I'm not cartin' any more upstairs. Call for it when ye get your supper."

"Between garglin' and hot water bottles," said Chrissie, "the room smells like a chemist shop."

She got him out of the kitchen door and followed him into the dining room, where he settled down on the sofa, holding his feet out to the blazing fire. He watched her carry the coal scuttle and stick basket out to be filled again. Annie listened to the clatters of Chrissie as she clodded the coal into the scuttle and threw the blocks into the basket – sounds coming up from the cellar.

"*Long, long ago*," Annie said to the empty kitchen.

# CHAPTER TWENTY-FIVE

## Heavy Breathing

One of the boarders stood in the kitchen doorway holding his plate of porridge.

"I'm not very hungry this morning. I didn't sleep very well last night. In fact I haven't got much sleep all week."

"I haven't either," announced his companion, as he accepted his bowl of porridge.

"What's wrong with the pair of ye?" Annie quizzed them as they hung about, letting their breakfast get cold.

"Well, we hear heavy breathing."

Now Annie and Chrissie turned around from the cooker.

"Heavy breathing?" They looked at one another. This was not an answer they had expected. "Where does this 'heavy breathing' come from?"

'Did some of the boys bring girlfriends into one of the rooms?' The awful thought made Annie's face stiffen.

"Is it a 'snoring' sound?" Chrissie asked them.

"No it is just regular heavy breathing."

"How long has it been going on?"

"For two weeks now, and it goes on all night."

The young men took their plates of breakfast into the dining room, and left the women to ponder this occurrence.

"It must be loud, to keep those two awake. Do you believe them?"

"The only one whose bedroom is on their side is the Fridge

Man, and he wouldn't hear anything, for he is always sozzled."

"Would it be him?" asked Chrissie.

"I don't think so," Annie told Chrissie. "He snores and grinds his teeth and yells a bit, but I've never heard him doing heavy breathing."

After the dishes were washed and the beds made, the three women decided to investigate around the house. There was no sound like breathing. This situation was not a happy one, as these boarders would keep complaining.

"Should we go into the old graveyard," asked Chrissie, "beyond the small yard at the side of the house?"

"What under goodness is wrong with ye? What breathin' would come from there?" asked Evelyn.

"I'm not dressing up to go into a graveyard," said Annie, who hardly ever left the house. She only did so when well dressed, which included her hat and gloves and a small silver brooch.

"Just go the way you are. You look grand," said Evelyn.

"I'll put on a fresh pinny," said Annie. This crossover type apron was her house uniform. "I don't want to put my good shoes on: my feet are hot."

"Keep your slippers on."

"The pom poms are chewed lookin'," said Annie, gazing down at them.

"They'll do rightly. Come on – it's a lovely day!" Evelyn now wanted the excuse to go out.

The sun shone on them as they made their way through the gates and viewed the scene in front of them.

"There's that young chap, on the left. The Australian we knew during the war, before his plane came down."

"Those folk will not be breathin' much," Annie remarked as

they began to walk among the graves. "Would you look at that!"

"At what, Mother?"

Annie stood before a grave, reading the name of the occupant.

"I didn't know Rosie was dead, and there she is. It must have been quick. She looked so healthy lookin' when I last saw her."

"You can't go by looks, Mother."

Annie made her way along, reading all the names.

"I have some friends out here."

The sun shone on the trio, lighting up the bunches of flowers nestling at the base of the tombstones.

"What did they pay money for these bouquets for? Sure they wilt and die in no time...Would ye look at that one: the 'wash on Monday, put the cat in the barrel' woman?"

Chrissie stopped to gaze at the writing on the tombstone. *"Beloved wife* – she was never that. I wonder where the *sniff* has gone?"

"It's little odds," Annie replied as she found herself a seat on one of the old flat pieces of cement.

"Watch that doesn't collapse and suck you in," said Evelyn, as she went to sit down beside her mother.

"This makes a lovely family group. It's a pity we haven't got a camera. We could send it to the relations in Belfast and Canada. Sign it *'Thinking of you'.*"

The women rocked about laughing at the effect this would have on the faraway friends.

"They would think we had gone mad."

"Maybe we have."

They began to feel rested, relaxed. Annie said she could doze.

"Doze away. We'll shove you in somewhere."

Footsteps sounded around a corner.

"There's a man, we'll ask him," said Annie as she jumped up, knocking her bunion in the soft slipper against the sharp edge of the tombstone. "Och, its Sammy Harper. You care-take this place, don't ye Sam?"

"I've been here for some time, Annie, and it's a great place to be."

Evelyn thought this was an odd statement. It was definitely a graveyard, after all.

"Have you come to see anybody in particular?"

"No, Sam. We are here on a quest, to find out if the 'heavy breathing' our boarders complain about comes from here."

"You have come to the right place. We have a living 'heavy breather', but it's not on the ground, it's up in the church."

They all gazed at the old church, bathed in the sunshine. It looked innocent of any living thing capable of producing breath.

"I heard it myself last week," said Sam, "when I came to lock up the hall. It shook me as well. And I had to search around but I found the culprit."

"Was it some old tramp comin' in to sleep here?" Annie couldn't wait to hear.

"Look up at the belfry. An owl has taken up residence there, and at night it sounds like its lungs are like bellows."

The women were so pleased, but it did not sound as if they could stop this nuisance.

"Och, there'll be no shiftin' that beast," said Sam. "The vicar thinks it's sacred. It's here to stay."

They began to make their way back: there was dinner to be prepared, baking to be done and Evelyn needed to head for the shops. When the young boarders arrived at the kitchen door again for their plates of hot food, Annie began to tell them about the cause of the heavy breathing.

"We can't do anything about it, so if ye want to leave, it's OK by us," she said.

"No way!" the first one said, so relieved to hear what was making the noise. "We're happy here. We thought it was a ghost."

"A ghost! That was the last thing you'd expect here." Evelyn gazed at the faces holding the plates of stew. "Why ghosts?"

"Well, all those bodies in the graveyard."

"It's so nice there," Chrissie told them. "We are going to visit there any time we have to spare. We haven't anywhere to sit outside, and it's a lovely place. Don't give it another thought."

Later, as the ladies sat over cups of tea, they talked over their visit.

"It would be a great place to be buried in," Annie decided. "I'd be near the house and you two could visit me so, I wouldn't be lonely."

"You're not serious?" Evelyn looked at her. "Yes, I believe you are. Sure, you haven't got a plot there. We have one at the other graveyard."

"I know," Annie answered, "but it's a newer one. I don't like the way they don't allow surrounds, and they just mow all over the whole place. It's not friendly looking, it's not got such a cosy atmosphere, and I like to think about Sam working there. He'd be above me. I know the people there. They are all older people who knew me."

"Sam won't be there long," Evelyn told her. "He doesn't look too alive on his feet. He might be ready to join you."

"I don't care." Annie's voice got louder. "When you're older, you think about these things. Would ye ask the vicar, Evelyn? I'd even go on top of Rosie, if her family wouldn't mind. She was a spinster, and nobody will come after her."

"She's in earnest," said Chrissie as she talked it over afterwards with Evelyn. "I couldn't ask that minister. I don't think he has any more plots. This 'breathing' business has started a handlin' with her."

Evelyn washed her cup.

"That owl thought it was cosy, too."

# CHAPTER TWENTY-SIX

## 'It's our money'

"There's a letter here from a place called 'Inland Revenue'." Annie held the letter out from her, and was astounded at the effect the statement had on her two daughters.

"What do they want with us?" Chrissie got out. "Who are these people? I wouldn't take any notice of their letter. Rip it up! We're not big business; we work hard for what we get, little as it is."

Annie threw the letter down!

Evelyn lifted it up and read the name 'Evelyn Tracey'.

"Why me? Who told them about me?" asked Evelyn.

There was a silence in the kitchen.

"This is a quare handling," said Annie. She thought about the situation and money:

"We don't smoke or drink or go on fancy holidays. We keep our money in the wardrobe how do they know what we have?"

"They don't," said Chrissie, "and it's our job to keep it there!" She slammed down a saucepan.

"What do we do now? Treat them with indifference?" said Evelyn, exasperated.

"Aren't there men called accountants, who work with figures and such?" Annie was sitting now working away with her finger at a small pile of crumbs on the table. She was gathering them altogether and thinking about the wee pile of money they had accumulated. It was hard wrought for. It was theirs – look at the way they saved and made do with everything.

"I'll get the name of an accountant tomorrow," Evelyn announced as she viewed the letter on the table. "I don't want to touch it! It has come into the house with bother on its back. Put it up behind the clock where we can't see it, Chrissie."

One of the bank clerks told her about several men who dealt in money matters. They would have to travel to another town where people didn't know them. They studied the names of the three men, and had trouble deciding which one would be suitable.

"John's a good Christian name," said Chrissie.

"Thomas sounds a bit grand, and Charles is even worse," declared Annie.

"John it is then!" Evelyn was glad it was decided, and an appointment was made.

Then another problem arose: should they dress down a bit?

"We'll not wear good leather gloves, and house shoes might be better. I won't wear a hat," Annie announced, "and my grey hair could make him sympathetic towards us. Your coat Evelyn, with the fur collar, is too swanky looking; wear your tweed. Chrissie doesn't need to dress down. She's always sensible looking anyway. No leather handbags, gloves or jewellery, except for a watch."

They listened in amazement to Annie, who was planning the visit like a battle move.

"We won't go in the car, the bus will look better."

They arrived at the appointed office and viewed the plate on the wall beside the doorway.

"This is it. It's scruffy lookin'," said Evelyn. "Maybe we picked the wrong man."

"Maybe people don't come to him," said Chrissie.

"This hall mat needs a quare whack against a wall," Annie replied

"Never mind, Mother. Open the door," said Evelyn.

The hallway was even more depressing. The bottom half was painted a shiny brown and the top part cream. The linoleum had worn parts, while another door led into an office. The counter was littered with folders, books and all the bits and pieces that office people used. It needed a good dusting, Evelyn thought. So did the woman behind the counter. She just lifted her eyebrows at them, all the while typing on a big heavy typewriter.

"Have a seat."

No further conversation. The women looked behind them and saw a long polished form.

"Sit down, Mother."

"No 'hello' or 'good morning'. This is no place to conduct business. We picked the wrong name," said Annie, making for the door.

"Stick your ground." Chrissie got her by the arm. "We're here now. Sit down."

"It's as well we didn't wear our good clothes," said Annie.

Chrissie was none too happy either, but three bus fares had been paid.

Another young girl sat further along the counter, and she was typing away, her fingers flying over the keys. She was better looking, Annie thought, but she was not allowed to stop work, even for pleasantries. Did they not know that their wages depended on people like us?

The place had an old dusty smell. Somewhere they could hear a lavatory chain being pulled. Evelyn's eyebrows shot up and they exchanged glances.

"How much longer will he be? We have a bus to catch!"

The younger woman went into a back office and came back, settling down again to her typewriter.

"He'll be out now."

A tall thin man appeared, and motioned the women to follow

him. They grabbed at chairs in front of a big desk and tried to arrange them. Evelyn got Annie seated, and then Chrissie sat down. Evelyn just stood. The man behind the desk did not notice. He began to ask questions, addressing them to Evelyn.

"When did you start your business? What is your turnover? Where are your records, receipts?"

He sat back in his chair flicking paper clips into a cup.

This was more than the women expected. They only had the one book – the one showing the records of weekly payments by the boarders. All their groceries etc. were paid by cash. He even asked Annie how much she got as a pension. She drew herself up and told him that was private, nothing to do with him or their boarding house.

He had sharp features and a thin wrinkled face. When he asked the questions he skinned his teeth. Evelyn told him to write down what he required, and they got up to leave. They made their way past the office workers and out into the street.

"What do we do now?" they all asked.

As they sat on the bus there wasn't much talk between them.

"How do we satisfy this man?

"Where do we get receipts?"

"We never run up bills."

Back home they made endless cups of tea and pondered their plight. They did not know which way to turn, to go about satisfying this man.

"We'll think about it later," Evelyn said. She told the other two to get on with their work in the meantime, and she would begin to search the drawers for anything she could find pertaining to the boarding house.

A week later, when Chrissie was at the door cleaning the porch and sweeping the street, she left the door open too long. The dog shot past her, bounding out from the kitchen and she watched helplessly as he rushed across the road. The sound of the car hitting the body sickened her. Annie and Evelyn heard her scream, and joined her at the door. The car had stopped, and the dog lay on the road. The women were beside the dog, lifting its head and trying to get it to its feet. Annie looked up at the long legs of the man before her, and her eyes travelled up to the face, the sharp nose, and the skinned teeth.

'It's the Income Tax man!' she thought bitterly.

Annie had a rolling pin in her hand, but before she swung it at him, Evelyn pulled her arm back.

"I'll carry it into your house," he said, as he lifted the dog and walked in front of them.

"Put it before the cooker for the heat," Chrissie guided him, and he gently left the animal down.

The dog was silent, but the women's cries of "our wee pet lamb" echoed around the kitchen.

"Is he going to die?" Chrissie was on her knees, crying and stroking the dog's head.

"He flew out in front of me. I couldn't help it!"

By now the tax man was shaking and Evelyn began to make tea. Annie sat, her head in her hands, gazing at the wounded animal.

"I've sent one of the men for the vet, but the dog is coming round. His eyes are open. We were all taken up with this Income Tax thing, and were careless," Evelyn told the shaking man.

"Look", he said. "About your returns. I'll come over and help you get it sorted – the paperwork and everything. You don't need to come over again. I'll come to the house here."

The vet arrived and examined the dog.

"No bones broke, but he needs to be kept warm, and no exercise for a while."

He took tea and scones as well, and there was a sense of great relief in the kitchen. The thin tax man didn't look so bad when he smiled, and his nose wasn't so sharp.

"It will be all sorted now he's going to help," Evelyn told the others afterwards. "He says a book will have to be bought, and everything recorded. We'll always know how we stand."

Annie piped up that she always knew how she stood, when she looked in the wardrobe.

When they were getting ready for bed that night, Annie laughed, as she thought of the tax man and the vet, heading out of the door each carrying paper bags of home made pancakes and potato farls. Once in bed she settled her steel framed glasses on her small nose, rattled a brandy ball round her mouth and rested the open Bible on her chest.

"What'll we make for the 'morra's dinner?" she said as usual to Chrissie.

All was well in the world again.

# CHAPTER TWENTY-SEVEN

## The Wake House

Evelyn hurried into the kitchen to tell the others that young Jamie the bank clerk's uncle had died. He was the one who owned the old pub in the country. The other boarders were laughing and bantering about how rich Jamie would be now.

"No more kowtowing to that manager he's always complaining about. He'll be rolling in it."

"Lucky sod."

They crunched toast, swiped bread through egg on their plates and gulped down cupfuls of tea as they talked.

"They're like a crowd of animals," Evelyn reported to the women in the kitchen. "The dead man doesn't get a look in. No sympathy for the old, those ones."

Annie stabbed at a bit of bacon with her fork.

"None of them will go to the wake or the funeral, no respect shown."

"Would you go with me, Chrissie?" asked Evelyn, as she sat down to consider the situation. "We'd need to show some respect for the chap from this house. He pays his rent on time, and he doesn't clutter up the bathroom."

"Don't expect me to go. I never liked wakes and funerals. I'm too near one myself!" Annie told her. "Mind you, it was always a great way to hear the latest gossip, or for a widow woman to get another man. It always was a good night's crack, a wake."

She got a faraway look as she thought about the many deaths

she had attended. It was a good excuse to have a look at the way some women kept their houses. If it was a sudden death, the house would not be at its best. Things like ironing and washing could be seen pushed behind sofas and chairs. Windows not cleaned were hidden by the blinds being pulled down. The women would comment on this:

"Did ye see the dust on that tallboy?"

"No, I won't go," said Annie, as she came back to the present. "You two go and tell me all about it. He'll have to still pay for the three days he'll be away."

"We won't dress all in black, but you wear your good grey suit and I'll wear my navy."

Neither woman would admit it, but they were looking forward to the outing. They had little rest from their toil, and it was an excitement to get out at night to meet lots of people.

Evelyn got Chrissie to take out buckets of warm water to wash the car. They got ready in the evening. They each got their handbags ready, with handkerchiefs and house keys and mint sweets for the breath. Evelyn said these were so useful when talking up close to someone. If the other person had a tainted breath a sweet offered to them would solve this problem. Their shoes were cleaned and shone, as when they sat in a row, feet on show had to look spotless.

Evelyn dabbed cologne behind her ears. Some people had the awful habit of hugging and kissing when they met, and the ears were close to their noses. Chrissie didn't want perfume. When their gloves were smoothed on carefully, they were ready.

"You look great," Annie told them as she looked them over. "Don't be long. The hot water bottles need fillin' and my hand's not steady. I can't climb the stairs either, to put them in the beds."

Their car nosed its way out of the town and finally down the lane to the pub.

"Would ye look at that!" Chrissie gasped at the way the cars were parked. They were abandoned up slaps in the ditches and across gateways. "You can always tell there's a wake, the way the cars are piled around the place."

The two women made their way sedately up to the front door of the pub. Their faces had a fixed sad expression, suitable to meet the mourners inside. Usually some people stayed outside a wake house – mostly young people – to smoke, to talk and get away from the sober atmosphere inside. There weren't any people outside here, and nobody had been appointed to stand at the door to welcome the newcomers and guide them to the coffin. A blast of warm air met them. It was smoke filled, both from cigarettes, cigars and the big open fire laden with peats. It was bright inside; candles and oil lamps winked and glowed in all corners. People were packed in, faces glowing, laughter rippling and voices so loud that the women couldn't speak to one another. A big tray of cigarettes was pushed in front of them. Another tray filled with glasses and bottles was moving about, held firmly by a big heavy man.

"Drinks, ladies? No seats, but you can lean against that wall over there."

"Of course, it's a bar," Evelyn got out, "a free-for-all. Get over to that window sill. My good stockings are ruined. Where's our boarder till we speak to him and get out of here."

"Would you like to see the corpse?" asked young Jamie, soon after.

"We can't refuse," Evelyn told Chrissie, as the young bank clerk looked earnestly into their faces. He fought his way through the crowd to a small side room. It was crammed with seated people, the coffin in the centre.

"My gracious!" Evelyn exploded as she fought her way in. "The poor man stuck in here with all this cigarette smoke. Is that ashes on that satin lining in the coffin? They're using it like an ashtray. And that woman is balancing a drink on the edge."

Young Jamie, the deceased's only relative, had tried to arrange the wake as best he could. He had no any previous experience, and just thought an open house was the thing to do.

"Poor chap. He's at his wits' end." Chrissie patted his shoulder.

The undertaker sat near the coffin. He didn't seem to talk much.

"Of course not," Chrissie said to Evelyn. "What could he say? 'How are ye keeping, everybody well?' All would sound as if he was touting for trade."

Jamie whispered to them that the undertaker had offered to get a pink coloured bulb to reflect a warm rosy glow onto the dead man's face, to make him healthier looking. He also wanted to sprinkle perfume on the coffin material, in case the heat brought up an odd odour.

"I decided against all this," Jamie told them, "but I can't keep the people from sitting around him, and I wish they would all go home."

"You have a problem right enough," said Chrissie, patting his arm, "but I wouldn't like to try to shift this lot. We only came to show you we were thinking about you, and we'd better make tracks for home. Annie's on her own."

"You didn't even get a cup of tea!" said Jamie, distraught. He helped them across the room to the door. One burly farmer tried to put his arm around Chrissie.

"How's my girl? Do ye not remember me, Chrissie? This was the best lookin' girl an' the best dancer in the parish!" he announced to the people at the door.

Chrissie was crammed into his big chest, her glasses knocked sideways and her face scourged with his rough jersey. The women got out and stepped quickly to the car.

"Wasn't that a carry on?" exclaimed Evelyn.

"Joe Duffy. I haven't seen him for thirty years. The big red face of him with sweat, too. Our chaps aren't so bad."

"Isn't it a pity of that young Jamie?" said Evelyn. "What'll he do if a fight breaks out? We're well out of there."

Getting out of the car when they arrived home, Evelyn told Chrissie to tell Annie that she had missed some quare fun. Chrissie was already running into the house.

"Mother, you have never been to a wake like it. It was like a scene from Hell."

"How much will Jamie get, do ye think?" Annie asked.

"There won't be much left of the stock if the wake goes on for another night."

They sat around the cooker and told Annie all about the coffin and the ashes.

"And to think that we dressed up!" said Evelyn.

"That young chap will have learned a lesson," said Annie. "He let the world in."

"But how do ye keep them out?" asked Chrissie.

"A big 'HOUSE PRIVATE' on the door," said Evelyn, putting her cup down.

"I wouldn't want people to come, and look at me in a coffin," Annie whined.

"Don't start that at this time of night," said Evelyn.

"Where would ye put me?" Annie asked, now thoroughly depressed.

"In the cellar!" Chrissie told her as she started to fill the hot water bottles. "Here, get your bottle and head off to bed. You're not ready to go yet, and we'll worry about where to put you when the time comes."

# CHAPTER TWENTY-EIGHT

## 'Where is she now?'

Annie had never been in hospital and had a great fear of doctors. A sore knee was rubbed with liniment or wrapped round with a cabbage leaf. The pain in the joint made her fear that her time had come.

"What if I canny use my legs and canny walk?"

Another cabbage leaf would be applied and she would whinge and moan, gazing at the floor and not looking up. A chest discomfort was diagnosed as angina by the doctor, and phenobarbitone tablets were prescribed for her. Every night at 7pm she had a pain and the scrabble for her tablets began.

"Where did you leave them Mother?" Evelyn's voice was sharp with worry.

"Are they not on the dresser?" Annie's voice was weak.

"You're not going to die just yet, if we can get the pills."

Evelyn and Chrissie tried to jolly her along.

"Look in your apron pocket. There they are – the bottle's stuck with brandy balls. Such a mess."

"Never mind the mess! Give me a tablet."

Annie would put her wrinkled hand out for the pill and sometimes drop it.

"Och, the dog'll get it."

Chrissie and Evelyn would scrabble about on the floor searching for the tiny pill.

"I'm putting it into your mouth in future," Chrissie told her.

"No yer not! Your hands always smell of onions."

Evelyn decided to put it on a teaspoon, and Annie's wee mouth would pucker up as she closed her eyes and accepted her medicine. The gnarled hands were crossed over her chest, and the other two women always viewed her anxiously until she asked them for a cup of tea. Then they knew she felt better.

'Somethin's got to come to take me away' was Annie's opening conversation. Although they laughed and cajoled Annie about her demise, they were really worried about her. Annie was the kitchen part of the machinery that made that comfortable place. When they went out the house was safe in her hands. All troubles were sorted by her wisdom. She had always been there, demanding so little but giving so much. She had a simple belief in God.

"My soul will go to Heaven, but I don't want to go yet," she said.

There was an innocence about her. They always laughed about the time they had passed their old dog in the street as they made their way to church.

"He was performin'," as Chrissie described his action with a female bitch. Annie had walked past the animals, eyes straight ahead, swinging her Bible in her gloved hand. When they came home he was waiting at the door and Annie stalked past him.

"I didn't think that he would know anything about that, considering the way he was reared here," she informed the rest as she took off her hat. Evelyn and Chrissie hid in the scullery, giggling.

"And she had two weans!" cried Evelyn.

Chrissie punched Evelyn as she wound about, holding onto the sink.

Now most of the spirit was going out of Annie. She had taken to wrapping a shawl around her shoulders, and wanted to sit by the fire.

"You'll get red marks on your legs."

"What's the odds at my age?" would be the answer.

Annie's appetite was poor.

"Just give me half a cup of tea. I don't want much dinner – just hardly what you would see."

Toast was accepted, but it had to be soft. Potatoes laced with butter and a few scallions beside them were accepted.

"That has an odd taste," was her frequent cry.

"It's your mouth, Mother!"

"I don't want brandy balls any more – get me cinnamons."

They tried to tempt her with different food.

"You're worse than the boarders," her daughters would say.

She took to wiping her face with a handkerchief.

"I always feel so hot."

"Take that shawl off you."

"Then I'll get a draught."

They didn't like to leave her, so when one of them went out the other stayed with Annie. Her hand would go down to rub the dog's head, and she would keep on doing it. Evelyn caught her one time as she nearly keeled over.

"My head got light," said Annie. "I'm useless: I can't even pat the dog."

As they took on the heavier work load it wasn't easy for them to always keep an eye on her. She usually stayed in bed while the boarders' beds were made, and they would call to her about the weather, the state of the bed linens. She always called back telling them to hurry up, she wanted up.

One morning there was no reply to their remarks, and finally Evelyn went in to see what was wrong. Annie lay back against the pillows, her long plaits over her shoulders, the pink nightdress making her skin look so healthy. But she wasn't healthy. She had died.

Chrissie stood beside her and they didn't speak. Evelyn stroked Annie's forehead and smoothed the rough grey eyebrows with her fingers.

"What were the last words she said?" asked Chrissie.

"It was 'You'd need to mind the boys' dinner'."

"What will we do without her?" asked Chrissie, as Evelyn sat on the edge of the bed.

"Doesn't she look peaceful, and not like dead?"

"That's because she died in good health. She hadn't any disease, didn't *fail*."

They talked away, holding Annie's hands. Chrissie cried but Evelyn just sniffed as she looked at the face she had loved so many years.

"Nobody will ever think of us as this woman did."

The kitchen when they went down was empty to them. Everything was in place, but her chair sat facing them without Annie. The shawl was draped over the back.

"We maun go'n," said Chrissie as she wiped her eyes with the back of her hand. "The men will be in for their dinner."

"And we need to phone the doctor and the undertaker."

They couldn't concentrate properly, but got the meal ready. As each boarder came into the kitchen the news of Annie's death was told. The women were amazed at the depth of feeling these men had towards their mother. Some hugged them.

"I didn't think they cared," said Evelyn. "We seemed to be on one side and them on the other."

"I'll believe it when they offer to bring in coal and blocks for that fire in there."

Chrissie hadn't much 'brew' as she called it in this show of affection, but Evelyn said they were all really sorry. After the doctor had gone the two women went again to look at Annie. She looked the same, her brow smooth. Evelyn got out a nightdress and they made Annie ready.

"She always wanted to be laid out in this one. She even starched it."

On the day of the funeral the boarders had all arranged to attend the service. Each one took a turn at carrying Annie out to the hearse. They had no relations, and yet the stream of well-dressed men attending made Evelyn and Chrissie so proud. They had listened to them getting ready; bathing, brushing down suits, polishing shoes and fighting to get in front of the mirrors to sleek down their hair. As they got into the car behind the hearse, the women were so pleased at the sixteen boarders walking behind the hearse. Even the Fridge Man was scrubbed and well suited, his grey hair shining silver in the sunshine.

"We'll make them a good feed when they get back. They'll be hungry, and Annie would want them to get their fill."

"Did they ever starve?" Chrissie muttered.

They talked away so that they didn't dwell too much on the coffin resting in the hearse.

"What'll we make for their dinner?"